Gender Fraud: a fiction

"A gripping read ..." Katya, Goodreads

Impact

"Edgy, insightful, terrific writing, propelled by rage against rape. Tittle writes in a fast-paced, dialogue-driven style that hurtles the reader from one confrontation to the next. Chock full of painful social observations ...." Hank Pellissier, Director of Humanist Global Charity

" ... The idea of pinning down the inflictors of this terror is quite appealing ...." Alison Lashinsky

It Wasn't Enough

"Unlike far too many novels, this one will make you think, make you un-comfortable, and then make you reread it ...." C. Osborne, moonspeaker.ca

"... a powerful and introspective dystopia .... It is a book I truly recommend for a book club as the discussions could be endless ...." Mesca Elin, Psychochromatic Redemption

"Tittle's book hits you hard ...." D. Sohi, Goodreads

"*It Wasn't Enough* punches well above its weight and straight in the gut ..." Shefali Sequeira, 4w

Exile

"Thought-provoking stuff, as usual from Peg Tittle." James M. Fisher, Goodreads

What Happened to Tom

"This powerful book plays with the gender gap to throw into high relief the infuriating havoc unwanted pregnancy can wreak on a woman's life. Once you've read *What Happened to Tom*, you'll never forget it." Elizabeth Greene, *Understories and Moving*

"I read this in one sitting, less than two hours, couldn't put it down. Fantastic allegorical examination of the gendered aspects of unwanted pregnancy. A must-read for everyone, IMO." Jessica, Goodreads

"Peg Tittle's *What Happened to Tom* takes a four-decades-old thought experiment and develops it into a philosophical novella of extraordinary depth and imagination …. Part allegory, part suspense (perhaps horror) novel, part defense of bodily autonomy rights (especially women's), Tittle's book will give philosophers and the philosophically minded much to discuss." Ron Cooper, *Hume's Fork*

Sexist Shit that Pisses Me Off

"Woh. This book is freaking awesome and I demand a sequel." Anonymous, barnesandnoble.com

"I recommend this book to both women and men. It will open your eyes to a lot of sexist—and archaic—behaviors." Seregon, Goodreads

"Honestly, selling this in today's climate is a daunting challenge—older women have grown weary, younger women don't seem to care, or at least don't really identify as feminists, men—forget that. All in all a sad state of affairs—sorry." rejection letter from agent

Shit that Pisses Me Off

"I find Peg Tittle to be a passionate, stylistically-engaging writer with a sharp eye for the hypocritical aspects of our society." George, Amazon

"Peg raises provocative questions: should people need some kind of license to have children? Should the court system use professional jurors? Many of her essays address the imbalance of power between men and women; some tackle business, sports, war, and the weather. She even explains why you're not likely to see Peg

Tittle at Canada's version of an Occupy Wall Street demonstration. It's all thought-provoking, and whether or not you'll end up agreeing with her conclusions, her essays make for fascinating reading." Erin O'Riordan

"This was funny and almost painfully accurate, pointing out so many things that most of us try NOT to notice, or wish we didn't. Well written and amusing, I enjoyed this book immensely." Melody Hewson

" ... a pissed off kindred spirit who writes radioactive prose with a hint of sardonic wit .... Peg sets her sights on a subject with laser sharp accuracy then hurls words like missiles in her collection of 25 cogent essays on the foibles and hypocrisies of life .... Whether you agree or disagree with Peg's position on the issues, *Shit that Pisses Me Off* will stick to your brain long after you've ingested every word—no thought evacuations here. Her writing is adept and titillating ... her razor sharp words will slice and dice the cerebral jugular. If you enjoy reading smart, witty essays that challenge the intellect, download a copy ...." Laura Salkin, thinkspin.com

"Not very long, but a really good read. The author is intelligent, and points out some great inconsistencies in common thinking and action .... may have been channeling some George Carlin in a few areas." Briana Blair, Goodreads

" ... thought-provoking, and at times, hilarious. I particularly loved 'Bambi's cousin is going to tear you apart.' Definitely worth a read!" Nichole, Goodreads

"What she said!!! Pisses me off also! Funny, enjoyable and so right on!!!! Highly recommended." Vic, indigo.ca

Critical Thinking: An Appeal to Reason

"This book is worth its weight in gold." Daniel Millsap

"One of the books everyone should read. A lot of practical examples, clear and detailed sections, and tons of all kinds of logical fallacies analyzed under microscope that will give you a completely different way of looking to the everyday manipulations and will help you to avoid falling into the common traps. Highly recommended!" Alexander Antukh

"One of the best CT books I've read." G. Baruch, Goodreads

"This is an excellent critical thinking text written by a clever and creative critical thinker. Her anthology *What If* is excellent too: the short readings are perfect for engaging philosophical issues in and out of the classroom." Ernst Borgnorg

"Peg Tittle's *Critical Thinking* is a welcome addition to a crowded field. Her presentations of the material are engaging, often presented in a conversational discussion with the reader or student. The text's coverage of the material is wide-ranging. Newspaper items, snippets from *The Far Side*, personal anecdotes, emerging social and political debates, as well as LSAT sample questions are among the many tools Tittle employs to educate students on the elemental aspects of logic and critical thinking." Alexander E. Hooke, Professor of Philosophy, Stevenson University

What If?... Collected Thought Experiments in Philosophy

"Of all the collections of philosophical thought experiments I've read, this is by far the best. It is accessible, uses text from primary sources, and is very well edited. The final entry in the book— which I won't spoil for you—was an instant favorite of mine." Dominick Cancilla

"This is a really neat little book. It would be great to use in discussion-based philosophy courses, since the readings would be nice and short and to the point. This would probably work much better than the standard anthology of readings that are, for most students, incomprehensible." Nathan Nobis, Morehouse College

Should Parents be Licensed? Debating the Issues

"This book has some provocative articles and asks some very uncomfortable questions ...." Jasmine Guha, Amazon

"This book was a great collection of essays from several viewpoints on the topic and gave me a lot of profound over-the-(TV-)dinner-(tray-)table conversations with my husband." Lauren Cocilova, Goodreads

"You need a licence to drive a car, own a gun, or fish for trout. You don't need a licence to raise a child. But maybe you should ... [This book] contains about two dozen essays by various experts, including psychologists, lawyers and sociologists ...." Ian Gillespie, *London Free Press*

"... But the reformers are right. Completely. Ethically. I agree with Joseph Fletcher, who notes, "It is depressing ... to realize that most people are accidents," and with George Schedler, who states, "Society has a duty to ensure that infants are born free of avoidable defects. ... Traditionalists regard pregnancy and parenting as a natural right that should never be curtailed. But what's the result of this laissez-faire attitude? Catastrophic suffering. Millions of children born disadvantaged, crippled in childhood, destroyed in adolescence. Procreation cannot be classified as a self-indulgent privilege—it needs to be viewed as a life-and-death responsibility ...." Abhimanyu Singh Rajput, Social Tikka

Ethical Issues in Business: Inquiries, Cases, and Readings

"*Ethical Issues in Business* is clear and user-friendly yet still rigorous throughout. It offers excellent coverage of basic ethical theory, critical thinking, and many contemporary issues such as whistleblowing, corporate social responsibility, and climate change. Tittle's approach is not to tell students what to think but rather to get them to think—and to give them the tools to do so. This is the text I would pick for a business ethics course." Kent Peacock, University of Lethbridge

"This text breathes fresh air into the study of business ethics; Tittle's breezy, use-friendly style puts the lie to the impression that a business ethics text has to be boring." Paul Viminitz, University of Lethbridge

"A superb introduction to ethics in business." Steve Deery, *The Philosophers' Magazine*

"Peg Tittle wants to make business students think about ethics. So she has published an extraordinarily useful book that teaches people to question and analyze key concepts .... Take profit, for example .... She also analyzes whistleblowing, advertising, product safety, employee rights, discrimination, management and union matters, business and the environment, the medical business, and ethical investing ...." Ellen Roseman, *The Toronto Star*

more at pegtittle.com

Also by Peg Tittle

fiction

Fighting Words (forthcoming)
Gender Fraud: a fiction
Impact
It Wasn't Enough
Exile
What Happened to Tom

screenplays

Exile
What Happened to Tom
Foreseeable
Aiding the Enemy
Bang Bang

stageplays

Impact
What Happened to Tom
Foreseeable
Aiding the Enemy
Bang Bang

audioplays

Impact

nonfiction

Just Think About It
Sexist Shit that Pisses Me Off
No End to the Shit that Pisses Me Off
Still More Shit that Pisses Me Off
More Shit that Pisses Me Off
Shit that Pisses Me Off

Critical Thinking: An Appeal to Reason
What If? Collected Thought Experiments in Philosophy
Should Parents be Licensed? (editor)
Ethical Issues in Business: Inquiries, Cases, and Readings
Philosophy: Questions and Theories (contributing author)

Jess

Peg Tittle

Magenta

Cover design by Peg Tittle & Elizabeth Beeton
Formatting and interior design by Elizabeth Beeton

Library and Archives Canada Cataloguing in Publication

Title: Jess / Peg Tittle.
Names: Tittle, Peg, 1957- author.
Identifiers: Canadiana (print) 20220200351 | Canadiana (ebook) 2022020036X | ISBN 9781926891958 (softcover) | ISBN 9781926891965 (PDF) | ISBN 9781926891972 (EPUB)
Classification: LCC PS8639.I76 J47 2022 | DDC C813/.6—dc23

"Here Comes the Bride", "Let Me Entertain You", and "I am Eve" are pieces by Chris Wind (see chriswind.com, *The Art of Juxtaposition*), which is one of my pseudonyms.

A more complete analysis of *13 Reasons Why* (titled "13 Reasons Why: The Elephant in the Room") appears on my blog (pegtittle.com) and in *Sexist Shit that Pisses Me Off* (2e).

There's a scene in *Tootsie* (1982) that is surely one of the most unacclaimed scenes of all time: Dustin Hoffman's character, Michael, as 'Dorothy', makes a suggestion on the set, and the director dismisses it out of hand. As I remember it, Hoffman's face—conveying surprise, confusion, indignation—shows perfectly Michael's reaction to the absence of (and, just maybe, awareness of) the advantage/s he's been receiving just because he's male. The entire movie should've been about that. Just that.

It wasn't.

And so I wrote *Jess*.

1

He cried. He screamed. No one came running to attend to his needs, let alone his wants.

This isn't right, he thought. Improbable as that was for a newborn.

They just smiled at him and told him to *Shhh*.

They smiled at him a lot. More often. In fact, the mobile above his crib had happy faces. It used to have Lego bricks.

They also made eye contact more often. Spoke to him more often. Sang to him more often. In softer voices. It was nice.

Eventually, he smiled back.

But oh, was he handled! Being held, and cuddled, it made him feel ... secure, it enabled him to relax in the world. But the gratuitous touching— Sometimes he just wanted to be left alone. Didn't matter. It was as if his body was considered communal property. Common property.

And he was fussed over to no end.

"Such soft skin!"

"What lovely hair!"

No one told him how big he was.

No one told him how strong he was.

His mother put ribbons in his near-non-existent hair, which he pulled out angrily. She put him in frilly dresses, with too much … everything. She got so upset when he spilled something on them. But what did she expect? And at the beach, he had to wear a top that kept riding up his chest or slipping down over his shoulders, pinning his arms to his side—what was that all about?

They all praised his first steps, but then wouldn't let him go very far. "Honeybun, no, you'll hurt yourself!" It was infuriating. Why did they call him a toddler if they didn't let him toddle about?

Suffice to say, it wasn't like *before*.

+ + +

When he was two, his baby brother was born. He'd watched his father, and then his mother, turn the spare room into the baby's room, but he didn't understand why they'd done that.

"Baby here!" The crib would fit in the room he and Sarah shared.

"Oh, honeybun, Kyle's a boy! He needs to have his *own* room!"

At two, he could tell boys from girls. He just didn't assign any importance to the distinction. Though certainly, on some level, he understood there *was* something important about that distinction. After all, Kyle's room was blue and green; the room he shared with Sarah was pink and yellow. Kyle's room had spaceships on the wall; their room had princesses.

One evening when Jess said goodnight to his new baby brother, he tucked one of his dolls into the crib beside him, taking out the stuffed alligator to make room.

His mom objected, reaching into the crib. "Jessica, honeybun, Kyle doesn't like dolls!"

How did she know?

Then his mom took the stuffed alligator out of his dangling hand. Until then, he'd never had any toys taken away from him. Until then, the only toys in the house were girl toys.

His face scrunched up. He was going to cry. No, he wasn't. He wasn't! He did. It was okay to cry now. It felt good.

Every night, his mom read a story to him and Sarah. Now they had to wait until she'd read a story to Kyle first.

He didn't know the stories were different.

As Kyle grew older, there were other differences. Other changes.

Whenever Jess had trouble with something, his mom was quick to help him. Kyle was left, was allowed, to struggle.

At snack time, Kyle was often given a second cookie. "Me too," Jess said, reaching out for the cookie jar. "Oh honeybun, no, you have to watch your weight!"

On Saturdays, his mom took them to the park to play. Kyle wasn't reprimanded when he got dirty, but Jess was. But how could you play outside and *not* get dirty? Maybe that's why Sarah just stood there. Is that what girls did?

One day, Kyle grabbed the dump truck Jess was playing with. To his horror, he let go. Before, he'd hang onto it. Or grab it back. Maybe even hit Kyle over the head with it. What was wrong with him?

Despite Kyle's aggressive behaviour, Jess wanted to play with him. At least, he wanted to play with Kyle as often as he wanted to play with Sarah. Kyle liked to play monster. Sarah liked to play dress-up.

He and Sarah got to do more stuff with his mom. He especially liked when they made brownies. The two of them took turns licking the big spoon after the batter was mixed.

Kyle, on the other hand, got to do more stuff with his dad. His father hadn't paid much attention to Jess even *before* Kyle was born. Now, it was like he was invisible.

And whatever they did, wherever they went, he kept being lumped together with Sarah—they were 'the girls'—even though he had more in common with Kyle. Actually, no, he didn't have more in common with Kyle. At least, not now. A lifetime ago, maybe.

2

Things got worse once he started school. He kept remembering stuff that seemed a bit … off. Not that he could put it in those words. Or in any words, actually. He just knew he was doing it all wrong.

He chose the wrong toys at play time. When they went to the library, he signed out the wrong books. He joined the wrong games at recess. When they lined up to go back into the school, he kept standing in the wrong line.

He didn't understand why it all mattered so much.

And he didn't understand Mikey. Mikey was a big boy with a crewcut. He was loud. And pushy. And he kept poking him. He poked him when they happened to be in the same play group or the same quiet time group. He poked him on his way to the blackboard. And again on his way back. He poked him when they were standing in line to get their jackets for recess.

"Stop it!" Jess would say. Again and again.

Mikey just laughed.

"I *mean* it! *Stop* it!"

Sometimes it was a really hard poke, almost a punch, but sometimes he simply touched him. Not a poke, just a touch. Here and there—

One day, Jess hit him. To make him stop.

"Young lady, you're coming with me right now!" The teacher's aide grabbed Jess and hauled him out of the class.

Straight to the Principal's office. He'd never been to the Principal's office before. He was a good girl.

Mr. Woodrow listened to Ms. Ellison's account, nodding. Then he sent her back to the classroom, but told Jess to sit in one of the chairs outside his office. "You wait right there, Jessica," he said sternly. "I'm going to have to call your parents."

His mother would be busy. She was always busy. She had to work during the day, and then at night she always had stuff to do. And his father, he wouldn't come. To school?

But, much to his surprise, both of his parents showed up. Within the hour.

"I'm sorry, Mr. and Mrs. Everett, but we have a zero tolerance rule about hitting."

"But Jessica doesn't— Jessie, honeybun, did you *hit* Michael?"

He nodded.

"*Why?*"

"He kept poking me. I told him to stop. But he wouldn't."

"Oh sweetheart, just ignore him. He'll eventually stop."

No, he wouldn't. He *knew* he wouldn't. Boys don't stop. They don't have to.

"Did he *hurt* you?"

"No, but he kept touching me. I don't want him to do that." Isn't that enough? Why isn't that enough?

He was punished. Told he couldn't come to school for two whole days. And his mother was very angry about that, because she had to give her shifts to someone else. She grabbed his hand roughly as they walked out to the car.

"You know, honey," his father glanced in the rear view mirror and grinned, "he's just doing that because he likes you."

Boys *hit* you when they like you?

Things were a little better in grade two.

Sometimes he played with the boys. He liked running around, exploring, doing stuff. But they were always shouting. And pushing and shoving. So sometimes he played with the girls. Except when they wanted to play princess.

But still …

When they lined up to get something, he saw the boys butt in ahead of him. So he did the same.

"No, Jessica, you have to wait your turn," the teacher said. Again and again. But he was tired of waiting for his turn. It never seemed to come. Now.

And whenever he drifted off on his own, the teacher called out to come back to the group.

At home, he got to read more; he wasn't always told to go out and play, to *do* something. So every week, he went to the school library to choose a few books to take home.

One day, Petey stomped over and grabbed at the book he'd just taken off the shelf. He held on.

"Now, Jessica, don't be selfish," the librarian chided as she walked over to them. "You have to learn how to share."

And cooperate. Girls were expected to cooperate. Always.

"That wasn't very nice," his teachers would sometimes disapprove.

He didn't recall it being so important before. To be nice. To be good.

One day, Jess had trouble putting the cover on a scrapbook. It had clips he hadn't seen before.

"Like this!" A boy took the book from him and put the cover on. "The teacher *showed* us!"

But the teacher hadn't. She hadn't shown the girls. She'd just told them to put the covers on and left it at that.

Another day when the class was on a field trip that involved walking to the local museum, they all had to wait and wait while a bunch of cars left a parking lot before they could cross and continue. Eventually, Jess screamed. Yelled.

"Inside voices," the teacher reprimanded. Even though they were outside.

"And it's okay," she soothed. "You're safe here on the sidewalk."

"I'm not afraid!" Jess retorted. "I'm angry! Why don't any of the cars just stop to let us cross?"

Another time, "Calm down," the teacher said, smiling.

She said that a lot to the girls. When they got angry.

And "If you can't say anything nice, you shouldn't say anything at all." Jess had said that the play the other students wanted to present that year was stupid. But it was! Even Andrew thought so!

On yet another day, "Jessica, would you please help Tony with this arithmetic?"

"No."

"Excuse me?" The teacher was horrified.

"I don't want to."

"But— Well—" She was so disconcerted, she almost stuttered. "That doesn't matter," she finally said.

When he was invited to Brittany's birthday party, his mom took him to a huge toy store to buy a birthday gift. As soon as they entered, she steered him to the girls' side. Jess wandered up and down the aisles, inundated with pretty and pink. He wouldn't want to play with any of what he saw. Would Brittany? Probably. She participated in all the Little Miss Beauty Pageants. During show-and-tell, she'd brought lots of pictures and two of her costumes: the evening-gown-and-heels and the bathing-suit-and-heels. She wore her tiara at recess.

His mother picked out something. Something pretty and pink and princessey. "Jessica, honey, how about this?"

"Okay."

Jess wanted to explore the other side of the store. Not for the guns or the monster ninjas. He actually didn't like playing with guns. Or monster ninjas. But he thought there might be something there that was more ... interesting. More ... challenging. He couldn't quite put his finger on it because he couldn't quite remember the chemistry set he'd loved when—

His mother reached out and steered him toward the check-out.

Then one day in grade three, the teacher read a new book out loud during quiet time. It was about a girl who liked to play with firetrucks, not dolls, a girl who would rather climb trees than play dress-up ... Jess *loved* the book. It was titled *But I'm NOT a Girl!*

The following week, the class had a guest speaker, a pretty young woman in a nice outfit. She looked like she came out of one of the magazines Sarah was always looking at. Ms. Gerson introduced her, then seated her in the special Speaking Chair in front of her desk. The pretty woman smiled at all the children.

"Girls, who doesn't *feel* like a girl?" Such an interesting question. Jess raised his hand.

"Boys, who doesn't *feel* like a boy?" Two little boys raised their hands. Jess raised his hand again, but when the teacher smiled and shook her head, he lowered it.

"You know what? That's okay!" the pretty woman smiled. "Sometimes we're born into the wrong body. We feel like a boy on the inside, but on the outside we look like a girl! Isn't that silly? Or we feel like a girl on the inside, but on the outside we look like a boy!"

Ms. Gerson smiled her endorsement.

"Sometimes things get mixed up," the young woman continued. "Isn't that right? Don't you sometimes put your right shoe on your left foot?"

Many of the children giggled.

"See?" the woman smiled. "It's just like that."

The woman talked for a bit longer, and then they had milk and cookies. They always had milk and cookies when they had a guest.

When Jess went home that afternoon, he told his mother that he was all mixed up.

"What do you mean, honeybun?"

He explained.

"Oh, no, sweetheart, you'll grow up to be a pretty girl, you just wait and see."

His mother thought it was just a phase.

In grade four, his teacher called his parents to ask if they could come for a meeting.

"What is this concerning?" his mother asked as she sat in one of the three chairs arranged in front of the Principal's desk. Jess sat in the chair beside her, and his father took the remaining chair. After moving it a bit. Away. As if he needed more space. Or distance. From.

His teacher, Ms. Matthews, was on the other side, seated beside the Principal.

"Jessica's grades are good, aren't they?" His mother glanced at Jess, then glanced back at the teacher.

"Yes, Jessica's grades are fine," Ms. Matthews smiled. "We're concerned about her gender socialization."

"Her what?" Jess' father spoke up.

Mr. Woodrow turned to her father. "We think your daughter could benefit from meeting with a counsellor a few times. We've prepared a list of therapists for you to consider," he slid a sheet of paper across the desk, "though I'm sure you'll find all of them to be—"

"You want us to send her to a shrink?" Jess' father was angry. "There's nothing wrong with our daughter!"

"But Todd," Jess' mother said to him in a calming voice, putting her hand on his arm, as if it were her job to control his outbursts, "you know she always wants to do boy things. She's been like that since she was little, you *know* that!" And it had been starting to worry her.

"Well, maybe that's because boy things are more fun!" He laughed.

"Yes," Ms. Matthews said gently, "but we have to ask why Jessica *considers* them to be more fun."

The conversation continued for a few more minutes, then Mr. Woodrow stood up, indicating that they had taken enough of his time. Jess' mother took the list, and the three of them went out to the car.

"She's just a tomboy," Jess' father said as he started the car. "She'll grow out of it, you'll see." He looked in the rear view mirror and winked at his daughter. "Just as soon as she discovers boys!"

The following year, the school implemented a dress code which stated that girls had to wear dresses or skirts. No shorts or long pants were allowed. True, the county had a reputation for having the most conservative board in the province, but other schools soon followed. In any case, it didn't affect Jess because that had already been his mom's rule. He usually wore a smock top and a plain skirt.

What *did* affect Jess was that the grade five boys wouldn't let him play baseball with them at recess. "NO GIRLS ALLOWED!" they'd shout, one even physically pushing Jess away.

But the girls just stood around in giggling clumps. Which was stupid.

So he joined a threesome that played catch. "Lezzies," the boys muttered with disgust as they passed them. Sadly, many of the girls followed suit.

Then some of the boys started laying in wait and when they saw a girl, *any* girl, on her own, by herself, they rushed at her, pushed her to the ground, yanked up her dress or skirt, pulled her underpants down, took a picture, then ran away laughing. The picture would be sent around until they got a new one. Of another girl with her dress or skirt yanked up. And her underpants pulled down. Jess watched for them. Every day. Whenever they were outside. And made sure never to be alone.

As his teacher had said, Jess' grades *were* good. By grade six, he was a straight-A student. But the teacher often passed over her raised hand, though often with an apologetic, embarrassed smile, and on some level, Jess understood that he raised his hand too often. But the teacher always asked "Who knows …?" or "Who can tell me …?" and Jess always knew, could always tell her. So it'd be a lie to pretend he didn't or couldn't, to not raise his hand.

If he'd been a bit more perceptive, a bit older, he would've realized that the teacher was acknowledging boys more often than girls. Yes, of course, maybe she was just doing her job, trying to bring everyone along, teasing out understanding where none was present, but she paid more attention to the boys in general. In fact, eight times more attention. True, they needed more attention, because they kept calling out without raising their hands, they kept butting in at line-up, they kept refusing to sit still when told to do so. Refused or simply couldn't? Jess remembered— No, how could he?

In grade seven, two things happened at home …

"Sarah, you're not leaving the house dressed like that! Kyle, don't forget your homework! Jessica, don't forget your lunch!" Every day, his mother seemed overwhelmed with the task of raising three kids. No matter their ages.

So one day he asked her why she'd had a third kid. Hadn't two been enough?

"Your father wanted a son."

The words slapped him in the face. He wasn't good enough? What could, what would, Kyle do that he couldn't do?

Oddly enough, given the conventional understanding that aligned active and passive with male and female, respectively, it wasn't a matter of *doing*. But he didn't understand that. Then.

A few weeks later, when his dad had to leave for a couple days, he told Kyle to look after their mom. What? Jess was older than Kyle. And Sarah was older than Jess. If their mother needed looking after, wouldn't he've told *Sarah* to look after her? And seriously, did their mother need looking after? *By a kid?* It didn't make sense.

So he asked his father about it. He just grinned. As if her question wasn't meant to be serious. As if *she* hadn't been serious.

She saw Kyle looking at her. A smug expression on his face. Already.

Part way through grade eight, he started asking people to call him Jess, not Jessica. Couldn't say why. Not exactly.

3

The following year, things started coming together. They also started coming apart. That's what happens in high school.

"Time to wake up!" Sarah rustled his bed. She was already up, showered, and in her robe. Clearly a morning person.

"What? What *time* is it?" It felt early. Too early.

"Six o'clock! We've got to get you ready!"

He sat up, groggy. "Ready for what?"

"Your first day of high school!" Sarah beamed at her younger sister.

But he was already ready. He had a new knapsack, notebooks, pens …

"We have to make you *pretty!*" She trilled the word and started to pick and choose among the many tubes and jars at her vanity. Aptly named. His side of the room had just a dresser and small mirror. "Into the shower with you. I left my razor and shaving cream on the counter. Pits and legs! We can talk about your bush later."

"What?"

"Go, go, go!"

Her enthusiasm was a little infectious. But just a little. He groaned, then got himself out of bed and into the shower.

"And use the conditioner!"

It took a while. Soap, shampoo, conditioner... Plus, he'd never shaved before. Had never shaved his pits and legs before. It took longer than ... He tried to grab onto the thought, but ... couldn't.

"And the lotion!"

The lotion was cherry-scented. He liked it.

"Okay, sit right here, my little princess, and let's see what we can do!"

Jess sat in the pink faux-baroque chair and faced Sarah's large mirror. And the seemingly even larger array of products spread out before him.

"First, let's do something about those brows of yours." She leaned in with a pair of tweezers.

"OW! That hurt!" In fact, a spot of blood appeared.

She plucked out another hair. "OW!"

"Oh, don't be such a baby. It only hurts for a second. You'll get used to it."

What? Why should he get used to something that hurts?

Ten minutes later he had— A quizzical face. She'd arched the brows somehow so they gave the impression of thoughtfulness. He kind of liked it. Even though it felt like a little like cheating.

Next, she spread some goop on his face, rubbing it in more than he would've liked. Then she put a different kind of goop on his face, this one she rubbed in with a lighter touch. Then she reached for a small tube and applied a dab here and a dab there. If he had to cover up his face this much, he thought, he may as well wear a burka.

"Take this one with you," she said, giving the last tube to him. "You can touch up during the day." Right.

Then she applied eyeliner, mascara, and lipstick, all the while giving instructions and explanations. As if she expected him to do it himself the next day. And every day thereafter. Like that was going to happen.

He actually didn't mind what the eyeliner did, or even the mascara. The eyes were the windows to the soul, and she'd added … depth, drama.

But what was with the lipstick? Was he supposed to appear ever ready to kiss? No, lips don't get red when you're ready to kiss. Do they? He was embarrassed to admit that he hadn't yet been kissed. Clearly he was some kind of freak. Many girls he knew back in grade eight had already 'done it'.

"Okay, now close your eyes," Sarah said. He did so, wondering for a moment whether he could open them again with all that gunk on. And she was putting on more?

"Ta-dah!"

He looked at the outfit she was holding on display.

"My gift," she smiled. "For your first day!"

It was a flouncy skirt and a tight little blouse. Not what he would have chosen. At all. But what could he say?

"Thanks." He took it from her and started putting it on. He fumbled with the blouse. The buttons were on the wrong side. Wait, how— And why would—

"No," she said as he reached for his knee socks, "here." She handed him a new package of panty hose.

He felt exposed wearing a skirt and knee socks, and often cold, but wearing panty hose was worse. And took forever to get on without it feeling twisty. Finally done, he reached for his penny loafers, but Sarah swooped in and took them out of his hands.

"Not today! Here!" She'd gotten Jess' dress shoes out of her closet.

"But these are for—"

"Your first day of high school *is* a special occasion. It's okay, I cleared it with Mom."

She and Mom had talked about this? It felt like a conspiracy.

Reluctantly, Jess took the shoes and headed out the bedroom door. He'd break a leg if he tried to go down the stairs in them.

"Wait!" Sarah cried out and reached into her jewelry box. Jess had a jewelry box too—it was a birthday gift, along with the brush-comb-and-mirror set he never used—but it was mostly empty. He had a couple bracelets, one a gold chain, the other a leather braid, but Sarah and his Mom had pronounced both of them inappropriate. For what?

The necklace Sarah had chosen was okay, but the earrings were way too tight.

"If you get your ears pierced, you wouldn't have to wear clip-ons," she said, repositioning them a bit to make sure they were both centered.

The logic troubled him. Why not just not wear earrings?

He headed toward the door again. Once downstairs, he poured himself a bowl of cereal and put a slice of bread in the toaster.

"No time!" Sarah nodded to the clock. "You need to cut back anyway."

He looked at her with puzzlement.

"That skirt is a size eight!"

The number meant nothing to him. Should it?

He grunted, then went to the closet for his jacket.

"And don't forget to keep your tummy tucked in," Sarah said as she watched him walk across the room.

He turned to stare at her.

"I'm your sister, Jessica, but you look like a slob with your stomach out like that."

He took a deep breath, pulling in his stomach. Was he supposed to keep his abdominal muscles contracted all day?

He didn't know, yet, about the Kegel exercises he was supposed to do.

Sarah wasn't satisfied. "We should get you some Spanx."

He didn't want to ask.

"It's basically a body girdle. You'll look great!"

He found his way to his homeroom, and claimed an empty desk near the back. Everyone who was already there stared at him. A few minutes later, he realized that that was where the boys sat. At the back. Well, so what. He didn't like sitting near the front.

His homeroom teacher, Ms. Kelly, seemed nice enough. She would also be his English teacher. Jess looked around the room, but saw no one he thought he could become friends with. But then, it was too early to tell. First impressions were unreliable, he realized that much. He recognized a few kids from his grade eight class, but they weren't kids he'd hung out with. In fact, he'd become a bit of a loner.

English, Biology, Algebra, then Lunch. He gravitated toward another loner at the end of Algebra, and once they'd gone to their lockers to drop off their books and pick up their lunches, they sat together in the lunch room. Maria turned out to be in his afternoon History class as well.

After a few weeks, Maria drifted away and eventually Jess saw her with a group of giggling girls. He wasn't surprised, really, nor upset. They didn't have much in common.

Around the middle of the month, he found himself making a note during announcements about try-outs for the football team. It jarred him. There was a girls' cross-country team. He joined that instead.

Even so, a couple weeks later, he went to a football game. Found himself sitting at ground level, as close to the field as possible. He missed— What? Again, he couldn't quite catch the thought, the memory …

He had Gym second semester. Usually, the boys and girls had gym separately, but for some classes, they met in the large gym together.

"Look at the stumps on that one!" One of the boys called out.

Jess was mortified. He ignored the calls as best he could, but that night he put on his shorts again and took a good long look in the full-length mirror Sarah had insisted on having on her closet door. *Were* his legs stumps? They *were* pretty much straight up and down, not tapering toward his ankles like the women's legs he saw in all the ads. But what could he do about that? He couldn't control the shape of his legs! He knew that guys didn't even *consider* the shape of their legs, let alone agonize over it.

Curious, Jess put on the dress shoes he'd stopped wearing early on. Ah. He saw now why women wore heels. They lengthened the leg. Tightened the calf muscle. Made the ankle look thinner. But of course he couldn't wear heels in gym even if he wanted to. Which he didn't. He kicked them off and put his penny loafers back on.

Maybe he could convince his Mom to let him wear pants to school. Not likely. He'd have to expose his stumps to the entire student body every day, all day.

He thought about organizing a bunch of girls to comment on boys' appearance. On things *they* couldn't control. "Look, that one has knobby knees!" "That one has thick wrists!"

Quite apart from what gave boys the right to judge girls' appearance in the first place? An image suddenly flitted through his mind: holding up score cards as young women passed by a men's dorm... *What the hell?*

One day, as he was leaving History class, the last to leave, thank God, his insides suddenly clenched and he doubled over, crying out.

"Call 9-1-1," he managed to say to the teacher, Ms. Tremblay, as his—bowels? No, that wasn't quite— Was it his appendix? *Something* was ripping apart inside.

"Oh, don't be silly," Ms. Tremblay chided, though there was a kindness, a sympathy, in her voice. "Surely it's just— Your time of the month?"

What? He doubled over again, with a sharp intake of breath. Feeling a bit of dampness, he rushed to the washroom as best he could, and went into a stall. Yes, it was blood. But— So what he was feeling— These were the so-called cramps that every woman he'd ever known had felt?

Pain sliced through his gut again, and he gasped. Almost started panting. He felt vaguely nauseous. This was going to last for *five* days? And he'd have to go through this *every month?* It was unthinkable.

"Caught you off-guard, did it?" Ms. Tremblay had followed him into the washroom. He heard coins clatter through the dispenser on the wall, the sound of a package dropping out, and then he saw her hand reaching under the door. "Here you go, dear."

He fumbled, he fiddled, he cursed ... A frustrating fifteen minutes later, he emerged from the washroom, and went straight home.

He washed out his clothes, then headed to bed. Curled into a tight fetal position as his insides continued to wrench. How could this not be causing permanent damage? And how could there not be a cure for this?

After a couple hours, he went online. He found heating pads, chamomile tea, ginger ale, Midol. Which was just acetaminophen. Great. Well, at least that was in their medicine cabinet. He considered also trying ibuprofen. And naproxen. Maybe all three together. He couldn't believe this was the best science had to offer. For something so debilitating, so *regularly* debilitating, to half the human species.

"You'll get used to it," so many sites had said. That was not comforting. In fact, it was disconcerting.

At the beginning of grade ten, Jess was invited to a party. It surprised him and, in retrospect, he suspected it was sort of an accident. He'd just happened to be with three other girls when they were invited. But he went anyway. He was curious. He'd never been to a party before. Well, not—

It was pretty much what he expected. There was loud music, there were bunches of kids, standing around, talking, laughing, there was beer, and something fruity for the girls to drink ...

After a bit of wandering around, he joined a group of girls dancing in the middle of the room. It was fun, bopping around. And it suddenly— He'd never danced before. Yes, he'd shuffled around, slowly, holding a girl tightly to him, but it was more ... it was just public foreplay, really. Men never got to dance. If they had, if they'd danced like he was dancing now, they would have surely been taunted. "Look at the little faggot move!" With a jolt, he realized that that was the most complete memory he'd had to now. Wait—*memory?*

The music changed, and the girls switched from bopping to … slinking. They stuck out their boobs, arched their backs, swayed their hips, to the sexy moans of the vocalist who *wanted it now, baby.* They were advertising. He left the floor.

"Hey Ho!" a guy sitting on the couch called out and waved him over with his beer bottle. He smiled—a reflex—but it confused him. What he'd called him. Her. Yes, he was in a short skirt and tight-fitting cropped top—at Sarah's urging—but that's what all the girls were wearing. Had he overdone his make-up? He glanced in a mirror. He didn't think so. He ignored the guy.

But then one of the girls he'd come with nudged him. "Go on," she smiled.

"Go on what?" Jess asked.

"Go suck his dick!"

"What?" He turned to the girl with a look of horror.

The girl made a face and moved on. Away from Jess.

He just stood there. Confused, shocked, more confused— Then, not wanting to stand out, he started circulating a bit, trying to find someone he knew.

"Hey Ho!" another guy called out to another girl. The girl smiled, flounced over, then went down on her knees to suck his dick. All the boys cheered.

Jess stared. The guy had his hand on her head, to keep her from pulling away. When she gagged, they laughed. They *laughed.*

"It's no big deal," the first girl appeared beside her again. "You should try it. It's fun."

He didn't believe it. And it looked a little like the girl on her knees didn't either. But all the girls said they liked it. He suspected, now, that it was a way to save face. Because it was so clearly a humiliation. That's exactly what the boys made it. And they knew it. *He* knew it. He *knew* it. (What he didn't know was that there were 'fellatio cafés' in Europe where coffee and a blow-job might cost 50 pounds.)

But apparently there was no other way to become popular.

What did 'popular' mean though? Well, it meant that girls would be friends with him. It meant that boys would ask him out. Did he want that? Well, yes. He was tired of being a loner. And on some level, he knew that if he *wasn't* somebody's girlfriend, and later somebody's wife, he'd be invisible.

Of course, even if he *was* somebody's girlfriend, somebody's wife, he'd be invisible. But he didn't know that yet.

He started wearing less make-up. At the beginning, it had been kind of fun. And he could see that it was expected. Not wearing make-up was … shameful. That was weird. Because it indicated laziness? But men didn't wear make-up, and they weren't considered lazy because of it. So where was the shame? He couldn't figure it out. The moral undertones of it. Bottom line, he didn't like how it felt on his face. And he hated the time it took, the fussiness of it all. And he didn't like looking like a hooker.

Then one morning, he did it wrong. Apparently.

"Oh, look at the clown!" Justin had jeered as a dozen of them stood around the door waiting for Mr. Blummett. "Jessica's running away to join the circus!"

He marched into the washroom right then and there and scrubbed his face raw. He was so embarrassed. More by being reduced to tears by the boys' laughter than by mucking up his make-up.

"You should have told him he was butt ugly without a bit of make-up himself."

He looked up from the sink to see Shane standing behind him. A grade eleven student, he thought, but nevertheless in his grade ten Geography class. Shane must've been waiting like the others for Mr. Blummett to come open the door.

He liked Shane. She was quiet, but when she spoke, what she said was worth listening to. He liked even more how Shane looked. Strong, lean. He wished he had a body like that. He used to …

And no make-up.

And no blouse and skirt either. Shane always wore jeans. Torn at the knee. And boots. And the most interesting t-shirts. The one she had on at the moment—

"Who's that?" Jess nodded to her t-shirt.

"Taran Tula. You've never heard of her?"

Jess shook her head.

"You've got to get out more." Shane grinned.

"Yeah," Jess agreed with a grimace.

"Want to get out now? We can do you a make-over."

"No thanks," he continued to rub at his face.

"Well, we wouldn't use that shit," she nodded to Jess' open purse. "Do you even know what's *in* that stuff?" Shane reached in and pulled out his mascara. "Propylene glycol," she read. "Isn't that in antifreeze?"

Jess stopped rubbing. In horror.

Shane pulled out a little bottle of nail polish next. "Formaldehyde," she read. "Doesn't that cause cancer?"

It took all of two seconds for Jess to dump it all into the garbage bin.

He'd never skipped class before, but he certainly didn't want to go back. Justin would be waiting. With his friends. He'd be the Entertainment of the Day. He'd seen it happen before.

They went to the mall. Shane led the way to the men's section of the large department store they entered. Using the credit card his parents had given him for emergencies, Jess bought a pair of baggy cotton pants, with lots of pockets (actual pockets you could put stuff in), a large, loose t-shirt, and an equally large hoodie. Wearing the new clothes, he felt more like himself since—ever.

He transferred his wallet, keys, and phone from his purse into the pockets, then dumped the purse.

In an athletics store, he bought a pair of track shoes and a couple tight fitting sports bras. He'd hated the push-up bras Sarah had steered him toward on previous shopping trips. He had no desire to show cleavage. What in god's name for? He had always compromised by purchasing a padded bra. Though, alas, he didn't really need it. And the whole idea of *needing* to pad … The sports bras flattened his breasts to his chest so they didn't jiggle. He liked that.

He had pants at home, of course, and t-shirts, but they were for after-school and week-ends. Even so, they weren't nearly as comfortable as— Standing there, he suddenly understood why. Men's pants were way looser than women's pants. Given his thighs, now, they should have made things the other way around. And women's t-shirts had shorter sleeves, they kept coming untucked because they were shorter overall, and they were, of course, tighter. The hoodie was something new; he liked it. And he *really* liked the track shoes. He had sneakers for gym class, but these were more … substantial.

"What?" Shane saw the look of deliberation on Jess' face.

"I can't leave the house wearing this stuff tomorrow. Or the next day. Or the day after."

"So leave the house dolled up a bit and change when you get to school. Bring your new clothes in your knapsack."

"Can't. My sister, Sarah, will see me. During the day. Looking like this."

Shane considered that. "And what will happen if she sees you? Looking like this."

"She'll tell my parents."

"And?"

"My mother will disapprove."

"And?"

Jess thought it through. "You're right. It's not like she can force me. She'll be upset though."

"Wouldn't be the first time, right? Or, probably, the last. So …?"

"Yeah," Jess agreed. "But I'll probably get grounded."

He hadn't been going out at night anyway, so that wouldn't be a big deal. Wasn't allowed to. Go out at night. At least not alone. Wasn't allowed to wear earbuds when he went running either.

While they were eating pizza and sipping milkshakes at the food court, Shane took out her smartphone, wiped one of the earbuds, gave it to Jess, then played Taran Tula. It sounded like retro riot-grrls. The song was about— Of course! Shane was a lesbian! Did she think—? Was *that* why Jess liked Shane? Was that why Shane was being nice to Jess?

"Don't worry, you're not my type." Shane had seen the realization cross her face and gave her a way out.

Jess grinned gratefully, nervously. "I don't know whether to be relieved or hurt," he tried to toss it off. Unsuccessfully. "I don't know what my type is."

"Yet. You'll figure it out."

He tried to figure it out during the next cross-country practice. He thought better when he was running. Okay, so he wasn't a girly-girl. That much he knew. He wasn't like Sarah. In fact, all his life, he'd felt more like Kyle than like Sarah. Except that there was a lot about Kyle that made him uncomfortable. Thing is, he didn't know why, exactly. It wasn't that he didn't *like* Kyle. Though, often he *didn't* like Kyle. But there was something— It was more complicated than that.

He tried to put his finger on the emotion, the emotions, he was feeling. And that in itself was complicated. He'd never done that before—

There it was again. A sense of *before*. Of *remembering*.

He felt— He felt wrong. Because he wasn't a girly girl? Yeah, partly. But also because he didn't like Kyle. It was almost as if he didn't like himself. But he wasn't like Kyle. Was he?

No, how could he be?

He was like Shane.

No, he wasn't quite like Shane either.

He tried again. Who was he sexually attracted to? He was fifteen, he should be feeling some sexual attraction, shouldn't he?

Okay, yes, he— No, he wasn't sure. He couldn't separate attraction from sexual attraction.

Wait a minute, yes, he could. It's just that he wasn't attracted to who he was sexually attracted to. Hm. That would be a problem.

He thought he should be sexually attracted to girls, but he was actually attracted to boys. Thinking about a few of them made him … moist. Moist? Okay, that was new. Different.

Wait—different from what? And *'thought he should be'*?

There it was again. That familiarity. As if his body was used to something else, wanted to do, wanted to be, something else.

But he couldn't imagine dating any of the boys he knew. They were, in a word, obnoxious. Most of the time.

He really enjoyed hanging out with Shane. But what did that mean?

He decided not to think about it anymore. For now, he knew he didn't want to wear make-up. He knew he'd much rather wear pants and track shoes than dresses and heels. He knew he liked English more than Geography. He knew he wanted to run. In fact, he added a parenthetical, now that he didn't feel so competitive, he really *enjoyed* running. The experience itself, not the end result. Maybe all of that was enough for now.

"The garage needs to be cleaned out," his mother said one day at the dinner table. She looked to Kyle sitting on her left, and Jessica and Sarah on her right. Their dinner table seating arrangement had always bothered Jess. It made sense that his father was at one end, and his mother at the other, but why was Kyle on one side, and he and Sarah on the other? Because boys and girls. Everything had to be divided into male on one side, female on the other.

"Sarah, you've got your cheerleading tournament this weekend, I haven't forgotten," she added. "But the two of you," she nodded at Kyle and Jess, "can get the job done."

So next day, they got to it. Jess had always thought that men were detail-oriented. Certainly that's what he'd been told. But once he and Kyle had moved all of the big stuff out of the garage, Kyle considered his work done.

"Where are you going?" Jess called after him as he walked away.

"I gotta call Dave. Let me know when you're done, and I'll help you move everything back in!"

"What? You're not supposed to *help* me do this," Jess protested, "you're supposed to *do* it. We're supposed to do it *together. All of it* together." But it didn't really surprise him that

Kyle had assumed that the cleaning part of it—wiping the grime off all of the no-longer-used toys, the patio chairs, and the garden decorations, then brushing off the shelves, then sweeping the floor—would be done by Jess. By Jess alone. After all, he and Sarah had been doing the dishes, some of the laundry, the dusting, and the vacuuming since they were ten.

And, but, it wasn't just that it *was* cleaning work. It was also fussy work, *detailed* work: when Jess did the dusting, not only did he have to wipe the table tops and counter tops and window sills, he also had to pick up every bloody knick-knack in the house and run the dust cloth along every groove on every bloody knick-knack in the house—*and* crawl under the dining room table and run the dust cloth along every bloody chair leg and cross piece.

Standing in the middle of the garage, Jess looked around him with despair. It would take an hour just to clear the work table for some space—to sort out the mess of screws and nails that covered the table and put them into their respective little drawers in the unit fixed to the wall. Kyle seemed blind to such tasks, blind to the little stuff, blind to the details.

It was the same when Kyle cut the grass. He just did the broad strokes, the easy part. Apparently it was up to Jess and Sarah to clip around the trees and bushes, to do the finickity stuff, the stuff that took twice as long.

What was the logic? Men are bigger than women, so they should handle bigger stuff? That included driving bigger vehicles, Jess noticed. His mom's car was smaller than his dad's. He imagined his mother buying a car that was bigger than his and laughed. His dad would probably buy a bigger-still car the very next day. And yet, men were surgeons. They were also biologists and physicists. Blood vessels, bacteria, atoms—you couldn't get much smaller than that.

Besides, men *weren't* bigger than women. Sure, according to all the ads and every movie and tv show he'd ever seen, they were. But they'd clearly selected the *smallest* women and the *biggest* men. Most *real* men had narrower hips, thinner thighs, and smaller chests than women. Most real men were *taller* than most real women, and they usually weighed more, but that was about it, really.

So why did Hollywood *select* the smallest women and the biggest men? Because men must be better, and bigger is better? But it isn't. Bigger can just be fatter. And in many cases, smaller is better. The firefighter crawling under a bed to save a terrified kid needs to be small.

Maybe men handled big stuff not *because* they were bigger than women, but *in order to feel* bigger than women. Because they stupidly *believed* bigger was better. Which was true in the case of physical fights, but— Actually, no, even then …

Part way through grade eleven, Jess cut his hair. And felt even *more* like himself. Shane was delighted. Sarah was horrified. And his Mom—

"But you had *lovely* hair! Why would you *do* such a thing?" she wailed.

"Because I like it better this way," was all Jess could say. He didn't have the words, the analysis, for the real explanation. Long hair made him feel more like a girl, more female. And being female, in our society, was not a good thing to be.

A few days later— Jess had been doing as Shane had suggested, leaving the house in a skirt or dress, then changing as soon as he got to school, but it was only a matter of time …

Sarah had graduated and gotten a job, but Kyle was now in grade nine. And he saw Jess in the hallway. Jess saw him first and made a dash for the nearest open room, but.

At first, Jess thought Kyle hadn't said anything, but a week later, his parents ambushed him with an appointment with a therapist.

"Hello, you must be Jessica," the neatly dressed, manicured, and coiffured woman offered her hand, "and Mr. and Mrs. Everett. Please have a seat," she gestured to the three chairs in her office. Once again, her parents flanked her. This time, Jess sat reluctantly between them. He did *not* want to be here.

"I understand that you do not want to be here," Jess looked up sharply, "but your parents are concerned about you."

Jess grunted.

"Can you see that they love you?" the therapist, Miss Dinelli, said to Jessica. "In their own way?" People said that to women about their abusive husbands. It wasn't the way Jess wanted to be loved. "They just want you to be happy."

"If I could wear what I want, I'd be happy."

"And you'd like to wear …?"

Jess told her.

"Is that it?"

"I don't want to wear make-up."

"Clothes and make-up. *That's* what you're upset about? Those are pretty superficial things, aren't they?"

"Yes! So why are they so goddamned important?" So *definitive* is what he meant.

He heard the sharp intake of breath from his mother.

"Sorry," he said to her. Then turned back to the therapist. "And I want to be able to swear." He grinned. Kyle was allowed to swear.

"Is there anything else? Anything more substantive to your complaints? About being a girl?"

Jess glared at her. "I'm not *complaining* about being a girl, I just—" He just didn't want to *be* a girl. No, that wasn't completely true. There were some things he liked about it. It was just that— What?

"I have to be polite all the time." He grimaced. Stupid example.

"Is there something wrong with being polite?"

"No, it's just—" What *was* it? Being polite was good. *Men* should be polite. *More* polite. "My mom always tells me that if I can't say anything nice, I shouldn't say anything at all."

"And?"

"It's—" He didn't have the words. The *understanding*. It was a way to silence women. To mute their opinions. Because she never said that to Kyle.

"I'm not allowed to be angry," he tried again. "I have to be polite even when the other person isn't entitled to politeness." That sounded convoluted. But it was closer to what he meant. 'Deference' wasn't in his vocabulary. Yet.

"And I don't like having to explain myself!" he summarized in frustration. Even though he recognized, again, that that was a good thing. *Shouldn't* people be able to, be expected to, justify their feelings, their claims, their actions? Yes, of course. It was just that he hadn't had to do it before. And it was hard.

"Before, when I—" No, he couldn't tell her that. She'd think he was crazy. "I mean *if* I— Boys don't have to. Explain themselves."

"I see. Well, all of this isn't uncommon, Jessica. Many people experience a kind of mis-match between their sex and their gender. It can be a source of great distress, and that's what we'd like to explore."

It wasn't so much a mis-match between his sex and his gender. It was a mis-match between his past and his present.

Though, yes, okay, now, there *was* a mis-match between his sex and his gender: he was clearly female, he knew that, but he felt— No, he just *remembered*— No, he also *felt*— He gave up.

"Explore how?"

Ms. Dinelli went on and on, but the long and short of it was that Jess had three options: talk therapy, aversion therapy, or gender correction camp.

Next day, when Shane saw Jess dolled up again, she knew something had happened.

"The mall?"

Jess nodded.

As soon as they got to the mall, Jess changed. Before she'd left home, she'd stuffed her other clothes into her knapsack for exactly this reason. They headed for a quiet spot at the food court.

"Back in a minute," Shane said, heading for their favourite pizza place. She returned with a couple slices of pizza, a couple chocolate milkshakes, and a couple Chocolate Brownie Thunder sundaes.

"My treat," Shane said. "You look like you need it."

"Yeah."

Shane waited. Jess took a bite of the pizza, then a long, delicious, draw on his chocolate milkshake. Then a big bite of the Thunder sundae. And then he told her.

"What the fuck is aversion therapy?" Shane exploded. Actually, she thought she knew.

"She'll show me a bunch of images, you know, like girls wearing pretty pink dresses, bows in their hair, and lipstick, I guess, then girls wearing jeans and hiking boots or something, and every time the image is wrong, I'll get zapped."

"*Shock* therapy?" Okay, she hadn't known.

"Not, you know—not like when they hook up those things to your head. I'd wear a bracelet, kind of like a dog collar —"

"You're not some animal!"

"It doesn't hurt much. She let me try it. It just —"

"Doesn't hurt, my ass! It might not hurt you physically, but it'd be doing serious damage to your psyche! After that, every time you think of what you really want to do, you'll be— Hesitant. She'll be planting a reflexive fear of your own desires."

Yeah. Jess hadn't been able to put his finger on it. But Shane nailed it.

"So you'll have to work extra hard, you'll have one *more* bloody obstacle to overcome, just to do what you want, dress how you like, God *damn* it!"

Shane took a long draw of *her* milkshake. And a big bite of *her* Thunder sundae.

"And gender correction camp?" she continued. "What the fuck is *that?*"

"I think it's like those old-fashioned finishing schools where young ladies were taught how to set a dinner table, which spoons and forks to use—"

"How to balance a book on your head—"

"Instead of how to read it—"

Shane barked like a trained seal. He grinned. He enjoyed talking to Shane. It was nice. It was new. Men didn't really ever talk to each other. Everything they said was code for 'I'm better than you.' It was pathetic, really. And incredibly boring. Now that he thought about it. Wait, what?

"How to snare a husband," Shane continued. "First, don't let him know that you're smarter than him.' Which means act stupider than him." She grimaced. "You know, sometimes I think it's our own damn fault."

"What?"

"That men feel so frickin' superior. They believe our bullshit."

She was right, Jess realized. Men *did* believe women's bullshit. About how smart they were, how competent they were …

"Actually," Shane said a moment later, "I think it'd be more like those Christian 'normalizing' camps. You know, the ones that tried to make gays and lesbians straight with deconditioning or reconditioning or whatever the fuck it's called."

"Deprogramming. That's what they called undoing the brainwashing done by cults."

"Who *is* this woman?" Shane asked then. "Is she actually a certified therapist?"

"I don't know. I guess so."

"Does she have a Ph.D. in … something? Emotional abuse, maybe?"

Jess grinned again. Sort of.

"And what the hell is gender anyway? It's bullshit. It's nothing. It's just a word we use to describe two sets of traits and desires arbitrarily associated with one sex or the other. It's certainly not innate."

Jess nodded. They were proof of that.

"Gender is how sexism is maintained," Shane said. "As Dee Graham put it, masculinity and femininity are code words for male domination and female subordination. Any intelligent woman will reject femininity."

Jess thought about that. Later, he would come across Lierre Keith who said something similar: "Femininity is just a set of behaviors that are in essence ritualized submission."

"You know," Shane continued, "all this trans shit became a big deal only when *men* started crossing the gender line. No surprise. I mean, women have been crossing the gender line for centuries: we've been assertive, even aggressive; we've entered so-called 'male professions'; we've chosen to wear unisex or men's clothing. And we've never felt the need to call *Newsweek* about it."

Jess grinned. She was absolutely right. Men thought everything they did was newsworthy.

"Feminists—*real* feminists—have been gender queer, gender non-conforming, gender variant, non-binary, whatever the hell you want to call it, since forever. See this is what happens when people don't know shit. Don't they teach history in school anymore?"

"You know they do," Jess grinned. "Just not *women's* history."

"Yeah." Shane took a long draw on her milkshake.

"So what are you going to do?"

"What *can* I do?" Jess said with despair. Then he shrugged with resignation. "I said yes to the talk therapy. We're going to 'explore and resolve childhood conflicts that have led to the wrong gender identification'."

Neither of them said anything for a while.

Then Shane spoke. "You've got to get the fuck away from those people. Your parents."

"Yeah, well." It would be two more years before he could move away. To go to university. Two years.

They finished their pizza and milkshakes, and, sadly, their Chocolate Brownie Thunder sundaes, then just walked around.

"Our carbon dioxide is at 450," Shane said. "We're past two degrees, and well on our way to three. And they're worried about pink and blue."

Next day, in the hall at school, he overheard a girl gush, "He thinks I'm cute!" and he almost stopped to correct her. He probably says that to all the girls, he would've said. Because he himself had once been that insincere. He'd never thought that the girl would actually believe it. He'd thought that she'd see it as the come-on it was. And either respond with a smile, which meant she was interested or— He shook his head. Took a few deep breaths. Focused on the here. The now.

And here, and now, he realized that Shane was only half right. About believing bullshit.

"That's not lady-like," her mom would often reprimand, gently, when he did something that felt ... normal. She thought she was helping with the therapy, helping Jess understand how to act like a lady.

But it wasn't that he didn't understand. It was that he thought the rules, for acting like a lady, were stupid. He couldn't just ask for what he wanted. That was rude. He couldn't just say what he was really thinking. That was rude too. He had to defer to others. All the time. No matter what was at stake. Apparently his primary objective in life was to not hurt others. Others' *feelings.* It was a new way of living. He wasn't sure he liked it.

The following week, Jess started looking for a part-time job. He was surprised to discover that even jobs were colour-coded: an after-school job at the hardware store paid more than an after-school job at Tim Horton's. But Tim Horton's was the only place that even gave her an interview. Good thing he'd started looking now, he thought. Two school years and two summers *might* be enough for first year tuition. He'd apply for a scholarship, of course, but he wanted a back-up plan. Because he *had* to get away.

It turned out that Shane had failed a couple courses required for graduation, so while Jess progressed through grade twelve, she retook those two courses. Jess helped her through. Honestly, they were both happy that they'd be heading to university at the same time.

But first, that last year of high school stretched out before them ...

And during that year, Jess started to worry that something was seriously wrong with him. He kept having the déjà vu episodes. No, they were more like flashbacks. Almost hallucinations. He thought maybe he was heading for a psychotic break. Or developing schizophrenia. It happened. He thought about telling Ms. Dinelli, then decided not to. She'd probably have him committed. He thought about telling Shane, but was afraid that she'd see him differently. Gender bending was one thing; mental illness was another. And God knows, as it was, he was struggling with how people saw him.

One day in Chemistry, Jess and his lab partner, Liam, were conducting an experiment. Their results were unexpected. They considered various explanations, but none of them quite fit. Then Jess hypothesized that the beaker had not been thoroughly cleaned, and it was the residue of a previous experiment that accounted for their results.

Liam said as much to their teacher.

"Good thinking, Liam," Mr. Killick said. "Given the experiments we did just last class, I think your hypothesis is correct!"

"Wait a minute," Jess spoke up. "That was *my* idea! *I* was the one who suggested that our results may have been contaminated by something in the beaker—"

"Just ignore her," Evan said playfully, "she's on the rag!"

Mr. Killick grinned at him.

"What?" Jess was horrified. "I'm not 'on the rag'! I'm angry! Because—"

"Yeah!" he laughed. "What I said."

To his dismay, Jess started to notice his breasts when he was running. Fortunately, this happened only a few days a month, but still.

Then one night, when he escaped into video games, as he had always done, he noticed all the big breasts. No, surely he'd noticed them before. Yes, but now— All of the women were in such skimpy clothing. And they were all just big breasts, long legs, and big behinds.

And they were all beaten up or raped or both, by the main characters. The men. How had he not noticed this before?

It was as if women existed *for men*. For their pleasure, for their entertainment, for their use— For whatever the men wanted to do to them.

And when the attacked woman cried out for help or cried out in pain— "Quiet, bitch! Shut the fuck up!" or "You worthless whore, you're fucking pathetic!" *How* had he not—

Ah. He was the 'you' now. That changed everything. He tried a few more games, but felt sickened—literally, he felt sick to his stomach—at what he saw. Woman after woman, fucked, beaten, spat on, killed, discarded. That was how men saw women, girls, him. Her.

Grand Theft Auto, Assassin's Creed, Hitman, Far Cry, Watch Dog ... He tried in vain to find something—else. Something that could give him the rush of power, control, agency, that he was used to getting from gaming. Without— Nada.

He found one game that had a female main character—but she had that perfect, so-called perfect, body, and it was almost completely unclothed. It cancelled whatever she was trying to do, trying to be.

He turned off the computer.

And never played another video game.

"Mom, sit down, you're not our servant," Jess said. His mother always walked around the table, dishing out everyone's food. They could just as easily pass the bowls and platters around the table.

"Oh, I know that, but your father worked all day…"

"So did you."

She just smiled. And truth be told, Jess hated her a little bit for it.

Then he decided to speak up about something else he'd often noticed.

"Why does Kyle get a bigger slice than me?"

Everyone stared at him. Her.

"I'm older, don't I need more?" In some cultures, men got not only the most food, but the best food. They ate before the women did.

"Men need more because they have more muscle," his sister explained.

"Maybe that's the effect and not the cause. Besides if you want to bring biology into it, as females, and the ones who will create the babies out of our own bodies, surely we're the ones who need more."

"Are you planning to create a baby any time soon?" Sarah mocked him.

He hadn't yet found "Trust Your Perceptions", and perhaps never would, as the blog would soon be taken down, but someone had pointed out that women feeding men was an appeasement, an international campaign to plead for niceness—Here, take this food, just please stop killing the children, okay?

His mother was right, of course. His father *did* work all day. He ran an advertising firm, and he often came home late. And he always came home exhausted, impatient, angry. At what, Jess didn't know, but he'd lash out at anything that upset him. They all kept their distance. Jess asked him once why he worked so hard. Why he didn't somehow make room in his life for enjoyment and pleasure.

"Somebody has to do it!" he'd shouted at him. "Do you think I *like* working this much? Who do you think puts food on the table? A roof over your head? I've got three kids to support!"

Yeah, Jess got that. But it was his choice to make those three kids. Didn't he know he'd have to support them? Of course he did. So why was he so angry about having to do so?

Jess figured that his father attributed his stress level to his hard work. More likely, Jess thought, it was because he treated everything like a competition. Whenever his father had to drive him somewhere, he acted like it was a race, a race he had to win. Every time a car overtook him, he got so angry. "It's okay," Jess would say, "let him pass. It's no big deal."

It was like cooperation hadn't even occurred to his father. In his mind, competition, competition toward control, was the only way to get anything done. Was he right? Had men *never* cooperated except under orders to do so? Or as a team, competing toward control over another team?

His father also probably thought he was doing the right thing because he was working so hard. But just because you're working hard, that doesn't mean, that doesn't say anything about, moral rightness.

But how did he know what his father thought? He gave a mental shrug. He just did. He knew that men's level of introspection, their self-awareness, was low. Men had little insight into why they did what they did, even into what they wanted.

That's why they were less apt to seek help—psychological, emotional, help. They can't explain their problems. They don't know what their problems are.

Well, in addition to it was emasculating to ask for help. Any help.

Regardless, his mother worked too. Surely she was contributing to their support. But it was as if her job, her contribution, her effort was invisible. It was—

Suddenly, his mental shrug slipped … into place. Oh god. That's it. *He used to be a man.* That's how he knew. That's why his tendencies, his expectations, were—male. For the most part. So, what, he used to be a man … *in a previous life?* So reincarnation— It *does* happen?

"So how's it going with the talk therapy?" Shane asked one day. "You're almost done, yeah?"

The agreement with his parents was that he'd do it for a year.

"Yeah," he replied. "A few more weeks. It seems I've finally convinced the therapist that I do realize that I have a female body."

"But it came with a male brain?"

"Not exactly …"

"You didn't tell her you were a lesbian, did you?" Shane asked, horrified. That could lead to worse problems. "Because that's not what a lesbian is. Male brains in female bodies—"

"No, I didn't tell her I was a lesbian. But— Look, can we postpone this discussion?"

Shane glanced at her, an odd expression on her face. "Of course."

"Where were you? I was worried sick!" His mother met him at the door.

"I was—" He'd gone out for a long run. And had stopped in the park. Because it was such a clear night, there was no moon, and the stars—

"It's almost midnight!"

He saw Kyle slouching in the doorway, a smirk on his face.

"You could've been—"

"Kyle stays out until midnight!" None of them had an actual curfew.

"Kyle's not a young woman!"

Right. Of course. He'd forgotten for a moment that he was more at risk of attack. Now. Well, more at risk of *sexual* attack. Because wasn't Kyle at risk of— Well, no. Unless they thought he was gay, he probably wouldn't be beaten up. And until he was older, he probably wouldn't be robbed. And Kyle was seldom alone at night. *That* was the difference. He remembered now. He was always with his buddies, he was always part of a pack.

"The sex gangs!" His mother wailed.

"What?"

"Kyle said there are gangs of men going around raping young women!"

Seriously? In Barrie? Why was this the first time he was hearing about this? He read the newspaper from time to time. There should have been headlines. Was it on the back page? He listened to his teachers. Why didn't *they* mention this?

And anyway, why should *he* be the one to change his behaviour?

Remembering the many times boys had criticized her body, it suddenly occurred to her: perhaps the right to criticize a woman's body derived from a right *to* a woman's body. And if men felt they had a right to *every* woman's body ...

And the right to the sexual use of a woman's body leads to, includes, the right to the reproductive use of a woman's body. Hence, no abortion.

Or is it the other way around: the right to reproductive use of women's bodies, perhaps thought to be grounded in the continuation of the species, leads to the right of all sexual use of women's bodies.

But women don't think they have a right to men's sperm. And hence to the sexual use of their bodies.

The following week, all of the girls were called to an assembly. It was the annual 'How to Avoid Rape' assembly. Be vigilant, be careful about where you go, and when you go …

Angrily, Shane glanced at Jess beside her, then spoke up. "How about you just tell the guys, 'Keep it in your pants'?"

Someone cheered.

"And," another girl shouted out, "tell them, 'Don't put any drugs in a girl's drink!'"

More cheers.

"And 'If you can't resist your dick, don't go out at night!'"

"*Or* during the day!"

Next day, when Jess walked into the school, she saw that someone had written on the general notice blackboard: "Women do not rape. End of story. If someone doesn't want to have sex with us, we feel sad and go home and write about it in our journals. Hypotaxis."

When it was time to apply to universities, Jess announced to his parents that he wanted to become a psychologist.

"That's nice, dear."

What? No discussion about whether that was a good choice? About which university to attend? It didn't really matter, because he'd already decided to apply to UBC and SFU. Toronto wasn't far enough away from Barrie. Still.

They'd already discussed which universities were best for Business—Kyle's choice—and Kyle was only in grade ten. Actually, now that he thought about that, he didn't think Kyle wanted to go into Business. Their *father* wanted Kyle to go into Business. So he could join him at his firm.

Their response was nothing new. No one had said anything when he'd announced that he'd gotten the Tim Horton's job. No congratulations on getting the job, no comment that he could've gotten a better job, no concern that the job would take time away from his school work.

It was like his aspirations weren't … important. They acted like he was just putting in time until— Until what? Ah. Marriage and kids. Seriously?

But he had no intention of getting married.

And he certainly no intention of having kids. He hated kids. Sarah babysat for a neighbour and once Jess had done it for her, because it was prom night. He vowed never to do it again. (Though he was glad that it had meant not having to deal with the expectations that he fuss and fawn over Sarah and the goddamned prom.)

"It'll be different when they're your own kids," his mother had assured him, when he'd confessed that he'd hated their whiney demands, their emotional outbursts, their relentless egoism.

Jess doubted that. But he hadn't, at the time, recognized the assumption that had prompted the assurance.

Whatever, he understood that his parents had no academic expectations of him. On the one hand, it was insulting. On the other hand, it was liberating. He enrolled in a double major program of Psychology and Gender Studies.

Shane, on the other hand, thought it was a great idea. "And that's a great combination! We focus so much on gender studies as a cultural or sociological phenomenon, but surely individual psychology plays a huge role."

Jess nodded. That's exactly what he'd thought.

"I mean, look at you and me," Shane continued. "We were exposed to the same cultural influences as all the pink vapourheads and yet … How do we explain us?"

Jess grinned. How do we explain us indeed.

"Are you still thinking about art school?" he asked her.

"Absolutely." Shane was into something she called new media collage art. Her YouTube videos were amazing. One of them, Jess' favourite, was a collage of what looked like home movies— the squealing engagement announcement, the dress-fitting, the bridal shower, the procession down the aisle, the reception and the speeches and the wedding cake and the first dance—all presented against a soundtrack of "Here Comes the Bride" with a voice-over enumerating the terms of the marriage contract through history, clearly indicating its origins in property transfer, and then the current statistics of wife abuse. The piece ended with the statement that 94% of all women get married. Shouted in silence with bold type on the screen, that fact then became covered, completely hidden, by confetti.

Shane had gotten a clerical job at an art gallery and was, like Jess, trying to save enough money for her post-high school dream. She had her eye on VanArts, a school in Vancouver specializing in media art. It was especially hard for her, because she'd just moved out. Her parents had never really accepted 'the lesbian thing'. That's what they called it. So Shane was supporting herself, sharing rent with two women who'd befriended her at a local GLBT meet-up.

Jess was offered admission by both UBC and SFU, but only UBC offered an entrance scholarship. It would cover first year's tuition, and it would be renewed every year for as long as he kept his grades up. So that's the offer he accepted.

"Congratulations!" Shane was happy for her. "I knew you'd have no problem getting in!"

A week later, Shane was in at VanArts.

"They'd be idiots not to want you!" Jess said, ecstatic about their future together.

They'd find a small apartment near the campus, share the rent, bike to school, and everywhere … They'd each find jobs to make that happen … They were both getting away, from their families, from Barrie …

They decided to celebrate by spending a week hiking on the Bruce Trail. The stretch between Tobermory and Dyer's Bay was supposed to be drop-dead gorgeous. They bought backpacks, hiking boots, a tent, and a few other supplies recommended by the outdoor store they'd gone to. Everything was more expensive than they would have liked, but they intended to make good use of it on the west coast.

Jess' mother disapproved. Hard to say of what, exactly. Women bearing a backpack? Women wearing hiking boots? Women hiking? God forbid, women being adventurous? Her father's response, as always, was no comment.

They took the city bus to the Northland bus station.

"Good morning, girls. Or should I say, ladies," the man at the ticket window smiled. "How can I help you?"

"You should say neither," Shane replied.

"I beg your pardon?"

"You called us girls, then changed it to ladies. Why don't you just call us people?"

Jess glanced at her. She was apparently feeling strong and confident … Maybe it was all the gear. Or the adrenaline of their adventure, the beginning of their new lives—

"What is it you want?" the man went from patronizing to irritated in a flash.

"I want you to figure out why you mention our sex every time you refer to us. Why is our sex so very important to you?"

Standing slightly behind Shane, Jess grinned.

The man glared.

"Two tickets to Tobermory, please," Jess stepped up. If Shane pushed him too far—

"You've never thought about it, have you?" She wasn't giving up.

"Nope," the man said as he took their money and passed them their tickets. "And I'm not going to. Next!" he called out even though there was no one in line behind them.

"But we call them boys, men," Jess said once they were outside. "Guys."

"Yeah, but somehow none of those terms is a put-down."

"Listen up, *ladies*," the voice was suddenly in his head. Coach. At half-time. He was trying to goad them to a better performance by ... insulting them.

"You're right," Jess said. Shane was absolutely right. To be called a female *was* insulting. Was *considered* insulting. By men.

Because to *be* female was ... to be inferior. According to men.

Their week on the Bruce Trail was wonderful. It was rugged going, but the solitude, the quiet— It was what they both needed. And every time they came to an overlook, they were absolutely stunned by the impossibly blue water, teal and turquoise and indigo, the expanse of it, the huge sky ...

During one of their many breaks, sitting on the sun-warmed rock, leaning against their packs, sipping from their water bottles, Jess came back to the conversation he'd asked to postpone.

"So I'm not dysphoric, and I'm not gay, but … I keep having these … flashbacks. It's like I *remember* being male." He held his breath.

"Like reincarnation? You think you were a man in a previous life?"

Wow. She'd gone there so easily.

"Well, thing is, I'm not sure I believe in reincarnation. Because if everyone were reincarnated, the population wouldn't be increasing, right? It'd be stable. We'd have same number of people, just—"

"Maybe in addition to the reincarnated … souls? minds? … there are new ones being created."

"Maybe."

"But then we'd have to explain why you're a recycled person," Shane grinned, "and not a new person. Karma? Is being female this time around a punishment?"

"Actually, I think it might be the other way around. I think being female is better, in a lot of ways, than being male. But my memories— I don't think I deserve a … reward. I think I was a normal guy."

"Which is to say a disgusting piece of shit."

"Yeah."

They stared out at the water.

"Maybe male bodies are becoming non-viable," Shane suggested. "I read that the Y chromosome has disintegrated into 'a trainwreck' of about 45 surviving genes. Down from about 2,000."

"Really? Maybe that's why male fetuses are more likely than female fetuses to spontaneously abort."

"And, or," Shane suggested, "we know that fetuses are female unless the Y chromosome, from sperm, gets to it. And sperm counts are declining. By 80% in just the last two generations."

"Hm. I didn't know that."

"*And* as much as 85% of it is abnormal," Shane was enjoying this, "likely to swim in the wrong direction." She couldn't help it. She burst out laughing.

"Didn't know that either," Jess grinned.

"The world's best kept secret," Shane replied, without the laugh. "Because."

"Yeah."

And then, after a moment, "Is all of that because of the chemicals in the environment?" Jess asked.

"Maybe. Maybe especially in the food men eat. Meat. Dead animals. Fed a shitload of god-knows-what … Growth hormones, steroids …"

Shane was vegetarian. Jess had become so, as much as was possible, living at home.

"Or maybe it's because of global warming," Jess suggested. "Heat is bad for sperm. That's why the testicles are on the outside of the body, right?"

"Right …"

The water was just so … *so* beautiful.

"How do you know you just don't have your old male brain, in a female body?"

Jess thought about that for a moment. "Because I'm not thinking about sex all the time."

Shane laughed. "Case closed."

And it was so nice, Jess thought. Not to have a sexual thought every eight seconds. He'd come across that figure somewhere. He believed it.

"And I don't feel as … driven," Jess continued. "And I definitely don't feel as … combustible."

"But maybe that's because you've got estrogen rather than testosterone coursing through your body. Not because you've got a female brain rather than a male brain."

"Could be. But a male brain would trigger the production of testosterone, not estrogen, right?"

"Yeah, but without the testicles to produce it—"

"No, we, female bodies, have testosterone too," Jess said. "Just not nearly as much."

"You're right. Okay, so it must be produced by something other than testicles. So … where were we?"

"Female body. Female brain. Now."

"Ah. Right."

Again, the water.

"Maybe your parents arranged a brain transplant," Shane suggested. "You know, like that thought experiment by what's his name, Williams? Shoemaker? No, wait. You said you *don't* have a male brain in a female body."

Shane gave it some more thought.

"What if we're in the future and you really fucked up and you're in one of those prison sentence machines that makes you *feel* like you're living years in hell when in fact it's just a few days."

Jess looked over at her. "I saw that in an *Outer Limits* episode."

"Yeah, *The 100* had something like that too. But," Shane reconsidered, "that doesn't explain me. I mean, I'm not some part of your private Truman Show. I cut myself, I bleed. 'Course, I *don't* cut myself, I also bleed," she grimaced. Menstruating on a week-long hike was a real hassle. To say the least.

"Plus, I wouldn't say this is hell … "

"So what exactly do you remember?"

"Most of the time, I don't have explicit memories. It's more like having strong expectations."

"Like you'd have after a lifetime of living as a male. Expectations of male privilege."

"Yes!" He turned to her. She'd nailed it. Expectations of male privilege. "And those expectations keep getting slammed. My experience, my *actual* experience, keeps surprising me.

"And," Jess continued, "it's like I have all these … habits. Like a couple weeks ago, I went out for a run at night. By myself."

"Habits or genuine desires?"

"It felt like a habit. As if it was something I'd just always done."

"But did you *want* to do it?"

"Well, yeah but—"

"So maybe you're just rejecting the socialization that says women *shouldn't* go for a run at night."

"But I'm not rejecting everything female. And that wouldn't explain the flashbacks. If that's what they are."

"Right."

They both stared out at the water again. In silence.

"Maybe," Shane suggested after a moment, "you're just crossing into another reality from time to time."

"I dunno. It's been like this since I was born."

Shane turned to him with surprise. "Really? Even as an infant?"

Jess nodded. "I think so. I think that's why everything felt … wrong."

"Hm."

4

Oddly enough, once Jess started university, the flashbacks became more frequent and more intense. As a result, more and more he found himself doing what he 'used to' do, without thinking. Often he was surprised, but more often, he was just angry: at the disjunct between what he had expected to happen and what actually happened—the disjunct between life as a male and life as a female.

At the same, to her surprise, there were momentary flashes during which she thought of herself *as* female.

Their university years flew by, as they do for passionate, intelligent, engaged people. Looking back, Jess saw a series of video clips, much like Shane's creations …

The first thing they did was find an apartment. It was a small apartment, but between them, they didn't have much money and they'd needed to pay first and last month's rent. It was, however, in the beautiful West Point Grey area, close to several beaches and the huge tract of relative wilderness that was the University's endowment lands. They'd been able to bring their bikes with them—they'd taken the three-day train from Barrie—and found that not only could they easily bike to the endowment lands, they could also easily get to Stanley Park.

They did both, often. They also explored many parts of the city, delighting in the many shops, the so many different things they saw ... Barrie wasn't exactly a hick town, but it was close, they now realized.

However, they soon found that if they needed anything fixed, they were put at the bottom of the list, and the landlord acted like he was doing them a favour. When Jess called him on it once, the man simply replied that he'd like to help them out, but there were other things he had to do. 'Yes,' Jess had replied, 'things like fixing the faucet on our tub! We're not asking for your *help*, we're asking you to do your job!' But then it took even longer for the man to get around to it ...

"Is it that they just can't wrap their heads around *working* for women?" Jess asked Shane, after yet another such incident. "They have to frame it as a favour, as helping out?"

"I'd thought it was that they're just so entrenched in the chivalry tradition, perhaps to the point they don't expect women to have money of their own, to be *able* to pay them, but I like your explanation better. It would also explain why they do a half-assed job most of the time. Backlash. For *having* to work for a woman."

"So, what do we have to do? Come on to the man?"

Shane laughed. "Well, I don't think *I* can pull that off, but you're welcome to try."

"Don't think so."

The faucet continued to drip, drip, drip. Of course, the finally figured out how to take it off (you had to pry the cap off first), took it to a hardware store ... and the problem repeated itself.

They gave up, wandered the aisles themselves, found one that looked exactly the same, bought it, managed to install it correctly. No more drip.

The next thing they did was find jobs. Jess considered consider calling all of the psychologists listed in the yellow pages, to ask if they would hire him as an intern, but then decided it was a ridiculous long shot. Shane was already an artist, so no doubt art galleries would love to hire her, and one did, but he hadn't even taken Intro Psych yet. Before, he would've just asked around, but now … who would he ask? His professors? The ones who, so far, didn't even acknowledge her existence?

So his first stop was Student Services. He stared at the job board. He hated kids. He especially hated looking after them. He'd make a lousy waitress. The Tim Horton's job had been bad enough, but at least he'd been behind the counter or at the drive-through. He wouldn't want to wear the uniform that seemed to be compulsory: short skirt, tight top, heels. It wouldn't be enough to be punctual and pleasant. He'd have to smile and flirt for tips to supplement the below-minimum wage pay that wouldn't even be enough to cover his share of the rent, let alone food, books … It would be demeaning.

And *there* was a topic for his Intro to Gender Studies paper: not just why women were paid less than men for the same job, because men and women so seldom *did* the same job, but why women's jobs paid less than men's jobs. Why were employers *allowed* to pay waitresses less than minimum wage? *Forcing* them to smile and flirt for tips …

The library needed people to shelve books, and the Communications department needed people to mark assignments for the remedial English course. He took a card for each of those jobs. There was nothing else.

Several professors needed research assistants, but those jobs weren't on the board. They went to whoever the professor approached (typically a male student; to approach a female student would be to court scandal) or to whoever approached the professor (typically a male student; most female students weren't so … assured of their capability).

He extended his job search to online. There were a lot of telemarketing jobs and a lot of customer support call centre jobs. Some freelance positions as content writers, a few tutoring positions. He ended up sending over fifty resumes. And then *another* fifty. He didn't remember it being this difficult … He also didn't remember to 'round up' his resume, inflate his achievements …

Soon after, Jess joined the cross-country team. There were more men than women on the team. Of course. The men were listed first on the university's website. Of course. The coach was a man. Of course. So was the assistant coach. Of course.

But that wasn't the worst of it. Just prior to their first meet, the coach distributed the uniforms. Jess stared at what was in his hands in disbelief. It was basically a panties bottom and a bra top. He couldn't imagine appearing in public so … naked. He'd tried on a women's bikini once, but even in the dressing room, alone, he'd felt so utterly self-conscious. It was tight and small and everything showed … Plus, he'd stopped shaving a while ago—it took so much time, waxing hurt, especially the higher up you went, and it was all about pornifying yourself for men, which she had no interest in doing …

"Could I have a pair of regular shorts and a shirt instead?" he asked the coach, handing back the two pieces.

"That's the uniform," he replied. "You'll wear it."

"No," he replied, "I won't. I'm not running 10k in a bikini. Would you?" He glared at the coach, then left.

"You're off the team, Jessie!" the man called out after her.

"You got that right!" she called back. He didn't need to be

on a team. He didn't need to compete. He didn't need to win. And with a jolt, he realized that all of that was true. He could just enjoy running now. More than he ever did before.

Shane was surprised when she came home early.

"Didn't you have your first meet today?"

"I quit."

"Okay … why?"

Jess told her.

"Yeah," Shane sighed. "Yet another way to undermine our competence."

Jess looked at her, not understanding.

"Having to wear a bikini turns serious athletes into sexual objects."

Ah. But—

"Can't we be both?" Not that he wanted to be a sexual object.

"You tell me. When you see— Before, when you saw a woman in a bikini—"

"Yeah." It was all he saw. It wasn't that the sexual trumped everything else. It was that it was the only thing he saw.

But who *cared* what men saw? *She* didn't!

Didn't she? She'd better. Because what men saw, what men thought, that was all that mattered. In a male-dominated society. Such as this one.

And as long as women were sexualized—and my god, but everything, every video game, every ad, every tv show sexualized them—men would see them as sexual, rather than collegial.

He thoroughly enjoyed his first-year classes. Psychology, Gender Studies, Philosophy, Sociology, and Biology. He started participating in class more than he had in high school, but so often, so very often, whenever he said something interesting, something important, no one took notice. Either that or his comment was somehow dismissed.

In some classes, she just stopped making comments. Nothing she said was interesting or important anyway. Apparently. It used to be …

Which is why he noticed that it didn't happen to the men. Not only were they not ignored or dismissed as often, when they were, it didn't seem to silence them. They didn't care. Which didn't— Ah. It was just words. Men participated in classroom discussions as if they were … certainly as if they were competitions, but also as if they were social events, games, entertainment. Which was, he realized, exactly what competition was. For men.

Needless to say, he found this realization—recollection?— about men's attitude to conversation horrifying. Words have meaning! And meaning is important! No wonder the world isn't getting better and better: the people in power aren't really talking to each other.

On the other hand, when his comments weren't ignored or dismissed, they were challenged. Aggressively. Almost invariably by one of the guys in the class. She was made to feel like he didn't know what he was talking about. Maybe she didn't, but why couldn't people explore each other's comments, elaborate upon them, refine them, move cooperatively toward something more cohesive, something more complete, something more valid? People would be more open and receptive then, instead of, as seemed to be the case, defensive; concession need not be an admission of defeat.

He soon realized that when there were only women in the class, that's exactly what happened. There were more smiles, more laughs, no pretensions of sobriety (men's cover, presumed synonym for intelligence). Even the frowns on faces were different: where the men were criticizing, evaluating in order to compete, the women were trying to understand, evaluating in order to improve.

He wondered though, whether, at its root, the problem wasn't so much the male obsession with competition as the male relationship to words. Women are better with language—he stopped, startled to realize this was so: she was more verbal than he was before—whether because of neurology or gendered upbringing or both, he didn't know; men are better with action, so it's said, again whether because of neurology or gendered upbringing ... So that could explain why women considered words to be important, and men didn't.

The phrase 'Sticks and stones will break my bones, but words will never hurt me' suddenly popped into his mind. What an awful lie. Probably first said by a man. Someone for whom words have no meaning. Or have meaning only as means to an end: what should I say to get what I want? Someone for whom actions speak louder than words. Another lie.

And yet, he wondered, if all of that were true, why the outrage at what Anita Sarkeesian had said back in the twenty-teens? Men had felt so insulted by her critiques of online gaming, her *words*, they threatened to rape and kill her. Apparently words *did* hurt. Apparently words *did* have meaning.

Furthermore, Jess noted to himself, despite men's relative incapability with words, they seemed to have an awful lot of euphemisms. Some men were so fluent with euphemism, they'd be hard pressed to be literal. Just as they were so used to bullshitting, they'd be hard pressed to be honest. (Yes, that was something else he realized. Now.) Ah. Euphemism was a denial of truth, a denial of true meaning. What if instead of 'Let's have a good time,' men *said* 'I want to have sex?'? If instead of calling it 'working out a yes,' they actually called it 'pressuring and threatening'? Euphemism was also, among men, code: a ticket to tribal inclusion. And so a status marker. No doubt the man who called their collective bluff and said out loud what they actually meant would be kicked out of the club.

Jess was also interrupted so much more than before. Sometimes it felt like being ignored, sometimes it felt like being dismissed, and sometimes it felt like being challenged. And every time, he stood his ground. He wasn't nice, he wasn't polite, he didn't defer, he didn't 'give way'. He continued to say what he was saying, sometimes interrupting himself to glare at the guy who was trying to talk over her: "Hey, dude. I'm talking. Can't you hear me?" The guy would turn to her with such astonishment. "I said, can't you hear me?" "Yes," the guy would recover, "I can hear you! Fuck!" "Then why did you start talking over me?" No response.

She would learn later that women were interrupted four times more often than men. (In fact, contrary to the stereotypes, men talk four times as long as women.) And that most of the interruptions are negative. And that men considered women to be dominating the conversation when they talked just 30% of the time.

He noticed that even when there were only one or two men in an otherwise all-female class, they dominated. He suddenly understood the appeal of women-only schools.

One night, while Jess was waiting in the bus shelter for the next bus—whenever it rained, she opted for the bus instead of her bike—she saw a guy heading toward the shelter, and for a moment, she considered leaving and then returning. That's what all the orientation material said to do. But damn it, why should he be the one to do that? He'd have to wait another half hour for the next bus. And where would he go? Who's to say the guy wouldn't follow? If *he's* the problem, *he* should be the one to leave and then return.

The guy entered the shelter and stood beside her. Not close, but … he *did* enter the shelter. Well, why shouldn't he? It was raining.

A minute or so of silence passed.

Then, "Are you *afraid?*" he taunted.

She recognized his voice. It was the guy who'd talked over her in class that one day …

He was taller, he was bigger, and, sigh, he was probably stronger. So, "Yes," she admitted. Then tore out of the shelter and ran.

Next morning, she moved the bear spray she'd bought for their hikes into the mountains from her backpack into her knapsack.

"Whatcha doin'?" Shane asked.

Jess told her what had happened.

Shane was angry. At Jess. "Okay, so you bearspray the next guy, and he comes back, with bearspray himself. Or worse, acid."

Jess froze. He hadn't thought of that. Why would he? "Well what am I supposed to do? Stop being out at night for the rest of my life? Let the guys in class interrupt me, talk all over me?"

Shane shrugged.

He was surprised. Usually she was a bit more … kick-ass.

"How much of a doormat do I have to be to survive as a female in this world?"

Early on, Jess decided to get some contraception. He was … curious. But still, no way, did he want to be an incubator. Or a mother. A father, maybe. No, honestly, he wanted his evenings to himself. So not a father either.

He'd initially gone to a drugstore, expecting to be able to get something off the shelf or over the counter. Nada. Everything required a prescription. Some even required physician administration. Well, *that* sucked.

So, prior to a visit to Health Services, he went online ... And was horrified to find out just how *much* female contraception sucked. Side effects for the combination pill and the patch included headaches, nausea, mood changes, breast tenderness, and, worse, blood clots, breast cancer, and cervical cancer.

Progestin-only methods were a bit better: he'd be in for weight gain, depression, body hair changes, and sex drive changes, but at least none of the life-threatening side-effects. Even so, this was the best they could do? In how many years?

The IUD was non-hormonal, but he'd seen too many pictures of developing fetuses tangled up in the thing. He wanted to stop things *before* the fetus. Before the embryo. Before *fertilization*. Plus you had worse periods with an IUD. His periods were bad enough. Also, an IUD cost several thousand dollars. True, it would last ten years, which probably made it cheaper than the pill. But he didn't have several thousand dollars.

A diaphragm? He'd have to go to a doctor and get fitted first. He wasn't keen on that. And he'd had so much trouble putting in a tampon those first few months ... what if he didn't put in the diaphragm right? And what if he was raped? Maybe if he went with a diaphragm, he could also get a Plan B packet in advance. Just in case. Because the abortion pill was no longer available, he knew that much.

He leaned back. All this just to have sex? Honestly, it didn't seem worth it. Even if he *did* have an orgasm, would it really be worth nausea, blood clots, and *cancer*? Highly doubtful.

But he wasn't going to depend on a condom. That is to say, he wasn't going to depend on a man. He knew better. He *knew* better ...

And *no* contraceptive was 100% effective. So he'd also be risking pregnancy. That is to say—he quickly went back online—he'd be putting himself at risk of nausea, increased urination, breast pain, back pain, swollen feet and ankles, fatigue, high blood pressure, diabetes, anemia. Death. Or abortion. Which of course came with its own risks. Cramping, pelvic pain, damage to the uterus, the bowel, the bladder ... Or just nausea, vomiting, fever, chills, diarrhea, and a headache.

He understood now, *really* understood, why 'screwing around' described sexual intercourse and 'you're screwed' described something about to go catastrophically wrong with no hope of remedy. Similarly, 'you're fucked'.

So every time, before, when he'd so casually— The thought jarred him. Well then why did the girls, women, agree to— Maybe they didn't. Not really. He couldn't actually remember what any of them had said. Which made him realize that it wasn't that 'no' was understood to mean 'yes'. It was that what a woman said, or did, just ... didn't really register. It wasn't really important. Maybe though, in his case, he couldn't remember because, well, he often couldn't remember the details of— Maybe.

He turned back to the decision at hand. He resisted his body's craving for pizza in order to maintain a good running weight. Surely he could resist his body's craving for sexual satisfaction. Should intercourse provide such satisfaction.

And then it dawned on him. Contraception, and abortion, were necessary only if sexual intercourse was necessary. And it wasn't. He didn't need sex. More to the point, men didn't need sex. He *knew* that. So all that fuss— If all those men—and it seemed to him that it was mostly men protesting outside the clinics, certainly it was mostly men who made the laws— If all those men didn't want abortion to be legal, didn't want abortions to occur, why didn't they just stop ejaculating inside women?

Despite the bus shelter incident, whenever the sky was just right, not completely clear but not completely cloudy, Jess went for a walk on the beach to watch the sunset. Because damned if she was going to let— She made a habit of getting there a bit early, to find the perfect spot. And he noticed, now, that most of the women left *before* the sunset. He knew why. Now. With shame, he realized that all that time, women couldn't enjoy the sunset, the stars, the night, in solitude—because of him.

Shane suggested that once a month, they borrow or rent a car—she'd obtained her licence back in Barrie—and head to the mountains or to the islands, to hike or to bike ... Jess enthusiastically agreed. On one such excursion, as they pulled into a gas station, they saw a man, an ordinary-in-every-way man, get out of his car and approach the attendant. Who had seen him approach and had stopped to wait, to see what he wanted.

Shane just stared. "Imagine going through life assuming people will pay attention to you," she said. "And being right about that."

Jess looked over. He didn't have to imagine. He could actually remember. Assuming exactly that.

Then, as the man returned to his car, he tossed something onto the ground. The way he did it— The way so many men just toss stuff— Jess had never noticed before. It was so ... 'I don't care'. About the thing tossed, about the ground being littered, about anything. To care is to be vulnerable. And a man must not be vulnerable. But it was sick, that attitude, that belief: to be a man is to not care about anything. (Well, anything other than tribe and status.) And it was dangerous. Not to care about ethics, the environment, beauty, pleasure, others …?

Over the course of that first year, they went to several of the islands, most notably Galiano, Salt Spring, and Saturna, they hiked part of the West Coast Trail, they went to Tofino … And they both decided to never go back to Ontario.

All too soon, first year was over. And although in the end, Jess did well enough to re-apply for the scholarship, it had been hard. He didn't remember trying that hard before. He didn't remember *having* to try that hard before.

Part way through his second year, Jess had the feeling she wasn't being provided with the same information as the guys in her class. She couldn't put her finger on exactly what she was missing, on what she didn't know—because she didn't know. For example, not only did most of the guys seem to know about research assistantships, they also seemed to know that you could take a look at previous years' mid-terms to see what questions were asked. Apparently the questions were recycled from time to time. Even if they weren't, it was a good way to prepare. They also seemed to know a lot more about grad school than she ever would. And yet, she'd never seen them in Student Services, perusing the job board or the grad school files or the career files … So how did they know? He couldn't remember …

Eyes opened by her courses as well as her flashbacks, she started noticing so many more … annoyances: consistent use by the professor of 'he' when 'they' was just as easy, lengthy, and condescending, explanations given to female, but not male, students …

She called out her professors on some of these things, but it didn't seem to help. In fact, it seemed to make things worse.

"You know what your problem is," one of the guys in the class she'd just left stopped her on her way to the cafeteria.

She'd automatically stopped when he'd addressed her. But then, appalled, he kept walking. How is it that men felt entitled to tell women what their problems were when they didn't even know what their own problems were?

A few months in, Craig, from one of her Psychology courses, invited her over to his dorm to watch a movie. It wasn't a movie she particularly wanted to see, but she'd wanted to get to know Craig a bit more. He seemed a little on the shy side, sort of serious, but also sort of quirky. They'd had coffee after class a few times, but Jess knew he couldn't just come out and ask him to, say, go hiking. It was a real pain, this little dance women had to do. (The one time he *did* ask a guy out, the guy had replied that he couldn't afford her. It took him a few seconds to realize that the guy had assumed she was a hooker.) So she said yes, thinking that such an evening might be less stressful than a full-out date.

She did wonder whether she'd be the only woman present. It was a men's dorm. He hadn't forgotten the many warnings in the Orientation material. Or his mother's alarm that one evening. In fact, especially given his sunset walks, he'd done a great deal of thinking about that. Because he'd had no idea that, before, that he'd been so … feared.

She was relieved to see that there were a few other women present, sitting here and there among the many guys. They found space on one of the several couches arranged around a very large flatscreen tv, then Craig went to a table full of refreshments. He brought back an assortment of chips, pretzels, and popcorn, and handed Jess a drink.

"No thanks," Jess said, "I brought my own." She pulled out a bottle of juice from his knapsack. He felt silly doing so, but it was what the Orientation material had recommended women do.

Craig looked insulted. And a little angry.

"You don't trust me!"

"No, it's— Well, I don't know you." Or, he should have added, anyone else here. She smiled, to soften— Then he caught himself, being so ingratiating, and wiped the smile off his face.

The movie started. They watched in silence. And she began to realize that maybe this *wasn't* better than a full-out date. For getting to know Craig.

Ten minutes into the movie, after several ads sexualizing women, and several trailers about movies that also sexualized women, when the captain of the ship, a man, of course, called the hurricane 'a real bitch,' Jess got up and left. Was there no end to the insults?

"Hey," he asked Shane when he got back, "why do you think men insult women so much?"

Shane grinned. "Did someone call you a slut today?"

"Not today, no," Jess grinned back. But it wasn't funny.

"Insult," Shane said, then continued as if she was reading from a dictionary, "Intent to humiliate and lessen. It puts us in our place. Our *inferior* place, our *subordinate* place."

"Yeah, but why are the insults always sexual? Bitch, slut, cow, ho, slit ..."

"Because that's the easiest way to put a woman in her place. Turn her into something sexual. Reduce her to her sex."

Ah. Right. The cross-country uniform thing.

So every catcall, every wolf whistle, every so-called compliment put him in his place. As a sexual object. He imagined explaining this to the next guy who 'complimented' him, but of course the guy would just stare at him, his mouth open, with total incomprehension. Of sexism, sexual politics, sexual objectification ... The guy would truly think he was paying him a compliment. It was what he himself had thought.

Though, wait a minute. No man who called a woman a slut thought he was paying her a compliment.

"But stud—that's sexual. And it doesn't reduce a man."

"No, it does not," Shane replied. Angrily.

"When men insult each other," he said, remembering, "we just call the other guy a loser." No. Not true. "Or a pussy, a douchebag ...," he trailed off.

Shane waited.

Right. Been there, done that. Being female was an insult. Because being female was to be inferior. An automatic loser.

Suddenly even the *idea* of rape— It was the insult of all insults. And it was such a unique humiliation. There was simply no parallel action for women to do to men.

"As to *why* men so *relentlessly* put us in our place," Shane continued, "you tell me."

Jess thought about it. "I don't know. It's just what we do. It's just ... habit." He'd never thought about it. Oh god. *He'd never thought about it.*

"The result of social conditioning?"

"I guess."

"Okay, but why are men conditioned to insult women?"

He didn't know. He'd never—

"Well, here's my theory. They insult us to put us in our place. Our inferior place, our subordinate place. Men are supposed to be better, right? Better than women. That's what everyone, directly and indirectly, tells them."

Jess nodded. That, he remembered.

"But they know deep down that if status were awarded according to effort, ability, or value, they *wouldn't* be better. They're insecure about their value, and rightly so. So they hang on like hell to their assumed superiority, their superiority by virtue of their sex. That's why they have to prove their *manhood* all the time."

Yes. That.

"So, since they need to be better as men, as *males*, so we need to be worse, as women, as *females*. And instead of going around all day saying 'I'm better!' or 'I'm good!' they say 'You're worse!' or 'You're bad!'"

Jess thought about that. They actually did both.

"Which," Shane concluded, "given, means going around all day saying 'You're female!'"

Ah.

"But isn't that circular? Subordinate, therefore our sex, and our sex, therefore subordinate?"

"Did I ever say men were the rational ones?"

That startled him. Because yeah, men *were* supposed to be the rational ones. But now … He was starting to see that they were just as irrational as women. Perhaps more so …

"Why don't women call us, them, on it?"

"They'd get angry. And hurt us. More."

Jess thought about that as well. Anger, lashing out, yeah. That *would* happen.

"Do you think they even *realize* they're hurting us? With their insults?"

"Did you?"

It took him just a second. "No."

He had been *so* stupid. *So thoughtless.* So ... emotionally-challenged. He hadn't been as bad as some, but still.

"Someone said in class a few days ago that we don't *expect* men to be sensitive to other people's emotions, let alone aware of their own."

"Nor do we expect them to be in control of their aggressive or sexual impulses," Shane added.

"Why do we have such low expectations of them?" Jess asked a minute later. Insulted.

Soon after, rather coincidentally, Jess started reading one of the required texts for one of his Gender Studies courses. *The Authority Gap.* It was a real eye-opener. Should be required reading for everyone, he thought. Because like the Martin/Nicole thing, a lot of men don't know how difficult women have it (after all, this is a meritocracy, so any advantage they have over women is due to their respective choices, their relative competence), but, maybe more importantly, a lot of women don't know how easy men have it. Because if they did know ...

He read about someone who, tweeting as Lady Alex, received rape and death threats. Posting the same tweets as White Dude Alex, she was retweeted, favourited, cited. That's what male privilege is, said James Fell. Being able to voice your opinion without getting rape and death threats.

Wow.

But yeah. Jess couldn't remember *ever* getting such threats. The worst threat he ever received was … Actually, he couldn't remember *ever* receiving *any* threat.

And the woman doesn't even have to be challenging male supremacy. As the author, Mary Ann Sieghart, pointed out, even if a woman is talking about pretzel recipes for godsake, she's threatened with sexual violence.

Hell, even if a woman isn't talking at all— In one study, fake accounts with female names that were set up in a chat room received 100 sexually explicit or threatening messages a day; accounts with male names received 3.7 a day.

Shane started reading the book too. They discussed what they read. One day, while she was reading it, Jess heard her burst into laughter. He inquired.

She'd gotten to the part about female reporters receiving threats of sexual violence. Sieghart had concluded with "What kind of person read through a newspaper and thought 'Hmmm. I don't appreciate Reporter X's writing. I think I'll send some hard-core porn-mail recommending a good, solid raping.'"

Jess cringed. Not that he had ever done that. But he knew she wasn't wrong. Wasn't exaggerating.

Half way through the year, Jess met with his Philosophy professor about a paper he'd written about Rousseau (who'd written about women as if they were silly children), asking why the man was still on the curriculum. Would some racist philosopher who claimed the intellectual inferiority of black-skinned people be required reading? He thought not.

But it wasn't the content of his paper that was the problem.

"Your writing is far too informal," the professor smiled at her.

"I don't understand—" He'd used correct grammar, punctuation; he'd consulted the APA Style Manual …

"Look, here," he pointed to his opening paragraph. "You use the first person. Throughout."

Jess still didn't understand.

"Instead of saying 'I think this' or 'I think that', you should just *say* this or that."

"But that would be presenting opinion as fact."

And that's how we do it, he suddenly realized. That's how men establish and maintain their superiority, their authority.

But, now, he couldn't even *imagine* having that much certainty, that much … arrogance.

Quite apart from mistaking opinion for fact, mistaking the subjective for the objective— *Is* it a mistake? Or is it intentional? After all, refusing to accept one's ideas as subjective means refusing to accept the possibility that they're incorrect.

Or, he thought, maybe the absence of the 'I' is simply the denial of, the failure to take, responsibility. Compare 'Your postal code is indecipherable' to I can't read your postal code': the first, without the 'I', doesn't even *consider* the possibility that the fault may rest with the reader.

Or maybe men just aren't that self-conscious. Literally. He had not yet read Owen Flanagan who had noted, in *Consciousness Reconsidered,* that "Insofar as reflection requires that we be thinking about thought, then an 'I think that' thought accompanies all experience," but had added, "There is no warrant for the claim that we are thinking about our complex narrative self. We are not *that* self-conscious." Well, Jess would think, when she got to Flanagan, speak for yourself. Your sex.

By the end of second year, his grades had fallen too much to re-apply for the undergraduate scholarship. No surprise, really. Twenty hours of work a week (he'd ended up with ten hours a week in the library, shelving books and doing other odd—i.e., simple and unchallenging—jobs, and about ten hours a week marking remedial English assignments) *plus* a full course load had finally taken its toll. He started to worry about being able to go to graduate school. He'd been thinking about pursuing the topic of sexism, teenagers, and tv ... If he quit his jobs, he wouldn't be able to afford it. But if he didn't quit his jobs, he most certainly wouldn't get a graduate scholarship to cover tuition.

What made it worse was that Kyle would be starting his first year in the fall, and he wouldn't have to work at all during the school year: his summer job with a construction company had paid enough to cover all of his expenses. In fact, Kyle had been offered every summer job he'd applied for. Every frickin' one. Six in all. It made Jess so angry. Kyle *always* seemed to have an 'in' ... She checked the bulletin boards for notices, she read the campus papers, and the city newspapers, but she never— She never seemed to gain the advantage Kyle seemed to have. Obviously, it was the advantage of being male, but how did that— Ah. Word of mouth. Guys told each other about openings. Guys hired other guys. Could it be as simple as that?

When she went to Student Services, again, this time looking for a summer job, she saw that there were a few yard maintenance companies looking for strong, young men. She'd done that sort of work before, so— Wait, no, that was *before*. She wasn't a strong, young man now. Well hell, she'd apply anyway. She could do the job, damn it. As she wrote down the phone number, she realized how shameful it was that looking after people's lawns paid twice as much as looking after people's kids. Did we really value our lawns more than our kids? No, we value what men do more than we value what women do.

Surprisingly, she got the job. She had to buy steel-toed boots—hard to find in a small enough size—but, given the pay, she could afford the expense without too much trouble.

The work came—she wanted to say 'naturally,' but … Certainly, it came easily. She liked being outdoors. She liked the work-out. Though it wasn't as difficult as men made it out to be, what with the self-propelled lawn mowers (only the senior guys got to use the riding mowers), the leaf blowers instead of rakes, the weed trimmers instead of clippers. She hated the noise now—yes, *now*—interesting … So she wore earplugs.

Even so, she heard them hoot and holler any time a woman walked by the property they were working on.

"Hey!" Jess said one day. "What makes you think you have the right to tell women whether they measure up to your standards, whether they please you or not?"

The guys looked her up and down. Slowly.

Another day, she heard, "Did you get any?" Certainly Jess had heard the question before, but he *heard* it now, really *heard* it, for the first time. The question implied sex was something men *got*, maybe *took*. *From* women.

And "Fuck!" Also *heard* for the first time. When, why, did the word for sexual intercourse become a synonym for anger?

When he heard "Are you hitting that?" he had to say something.

"We're not inanimate objects."

"What?"

"You referred to hitting women. Either you think we're inanimate objects or you're openly advocating assault."

"It's just a phrase."

"Don't be an idiot. Nothing is 'just a phrase'."

It reminded her of something she'd read in Cynthia Enloe's *Bananas, Beaches, and Bases: Making feminist sense of international politics*: women are experienced; they don't have experiences of their own. It was another way of saying we are objects, not subjects. Add to that what Kate Harding had said in *Asking for It*: rape is just the far end of the spectrum on which the other end is sexual remarks …

The crew often went out for a drink after work on Fridays. Even though it was clear that her presence on the job, her very existence, was tolerated, at best, she joined them a couple weeks in. She was curious about … her new perspective. As she suspected, she found the banter relentlessly competitive. And relentlessly sexualized. Hard to believe he ever enjoyed it, assuming he had, it was so one-dimensional.

One Friday, when Kevin stopped in the middle of some sexual tale the moment his girlfriend showed up, something new occurred to Jess. It wasn't because Kevin thought his girlfriend was ignorant of sex and therefore wouldn't get it. Or because he thought she *should* be ignorant of sex and therefore shouldn't get it. It was because he didn't want her to know that he thought of her, of every woman, all the time, as just a cunt.

A week later, Jess overheard one of the guys mention a new porn site he was all excited about. Curious, she went online and … it wasn't quite a flashback, but certainly a feeling of déjà-vu. Once at the site, she felt only disgust. Had porn changed since—whenever? What she saw was so … crude. Beyond humiliating, it was degrading. To both women *and* men. And boys started watching this at eleven? No wonder. The message would be quite clear. Women are for sex. They *are* just cunts.

He wondered why porn was still legal. Wasn't it hate speech, pure and simple? If a whole industry created and disseminated images of men being hurt, sexually, by women, women who apparently enjoyed hurting men, you can bet it'd be shut down in a minute. No questions, no debates, no exceptions.

Men say they *need* it. But *why* do they need images that humiliate and degrade women?

He tried to remember. Yes, he'd used porn. But had he *needed* it? It was certainly easier, quicker, to jack off with visual stimulation. So maybe if he'd had a better imagination ... Even so, did he need to jack off? And had he needed images of humiliation and degradation to jack off? He thought not. He hoped not.

The job was enlightening in other ways as well. Jess realized, or remembered, that men's kneejerk response was to make excuses. He saw it, noticed it now, again and again. In every conversation, whenever one of the guys was called out about something, he didn't even *consider* taking responsibility or apologizing. The reflex—and it really had become a reflex—was to deny and make an excuse. Only losers admit failure.

She also noticed that the guys got away with so much. She'd be working hard, and they'd be goofing around. No consequences. No surprise.

(And if they *did* get called on it, they'd get a second chance. She wouldn't've.)

Third year, she continued to enjoy her courses. In Psychology, she learned about Kolhberg's famous stages of moral development: ethical decisions made according to principles were indicative of the highest level of development. Jess, and most of the women she knew, achieved that in adolescence. They considered what was right, what was fair. So Jess, and most of the women he knew, were, among men, ethical geniuses. But that didn't make sense. Until she learned that Kohlberg had used only boys in his study. And yes, most of the men she knew used self-interest as a guide to behaviour. As he himself had done. Life was all about competition, you had to make sure you were one-up on everyone else, you had to make sure you weren't a loser. So of course you did what would *make* you, make *you*, one-up. He wondered if their obsessive focus on competition, one-upmanship, win/lose, saving face, reputation, perception explained *why* they seemed incapable of focusing on truth and morality. In addition to being so used to bullshitting. No, competition was the *reason for* the bullshitting. He suspected that most adult men couldn't even *define* good or right beyond their simplistic ten-year-old definition. Whatever that was.

Jess also learned that a great many researchers used only males in their studies. That's why so many women died of heart disease. The warning signs were different for women; even the experience of a heart attack was different for women. So, since most early studies had used predominantly men, not only were women unaware they were heading for a heart attack, even the heart attacks themselves were misdiagnosed, as indigestion or gallstones, for example. Furthermore, women respond to many drugs differently than men; certainly the dosage should be different. And so on. Women's experience of anything was, is, considered a subset, not a half-set.

Similarly, male bodies were the default for construction design. She remembered reading about a woman trying to become a firefighter, and she kept failing the test because the hoses were mounted on the wall with men in mind who, even if they'd been the same height as women and not six inches taller, would have had a higher center of gravity. She'd also read about women's inability to become truck drivers because they couldn't reach the pedals. Jess wondered whether her occasional awkwardness and sometimes outright difficulty using the lawn maintenance tools had been due to subtle differences in sizing.

When he started reading radical feminists—Beauvoir, Friedan, Steinem, Firestone, Dworkin, Morgan, and others, who recognized gender as the tool of subordination by sex and so advocated rejecting gender altogether—he realized his life had been, at least temporarily, hijacked by the trans narrative: if women had as much authority and freedom, as much personhood and humanity, as men, he wouldn't've even have considered the possibility that he was, or should become, trans. He would have accepted his non-gendered feelings and preferences as simply non-gendered feelings and preferences, not as an indication that he'd been 'misgendered' or whatever.

In his Women's History course, he read about the smile boycott. He understood it. Women were told to smile. All the time. Almost every day, his mom had said to him, 'Smile, dear!' She'd made it sound like a reprimand.

But smiling meant you weren't being serious. So you wouldn't be taken seriously. It was a way to subordinate women. He got that. But he liked being able to smile more easily. He liked not having to look stern, even angry, all the time.

"Come look at this," Jess called out to Shane one evening. She'd found a video showing two women in an iron man—yeah— competition. Helping each other make it across the finish line.

"It's such a metaphor, isn't it? Men disgrace the fallen, insulting and humiliating their buddies who can't keep up, who pass out, for example, when drunk."

"Women help the fallen," Shane finished the comparison. "We make sure our passed-out sisters get home safely, that is, without being hurt by men."

"It's like we're two different species."

Another evening, Shane was the one who called out. "One of these days someone needs to unpack *this*."

"What?" Jess asked.

"The 'adult image filter'. And 'adult videos' and 'adult magazines'. When did 'adult' come to mean 'male psychopath'?"

Jess grinned. Though, given porn today, there was nothing funny about it. Absolutely nothing. What was adult about coercing someone to do something she doesn't really want to do? What was adult about humiliating another person? What was adult about hurting another person? What was adult about doing sexual things to children?

Yet another evening, "This is messed up," Shane said softly.

Jess looked up from her own laptop.

"Feminist blogs are disappearing. First, it was *I Blame the Patriarchy*, but that was because Twisty lost the archive when she updated. And that was such a loss ... Then Femonade. Her *FactCheckMe* was another great blog. I think she just stopped. Exhausted. No surprise. But now ..."

"Now what?"

"I'm wondering whether they're been hacked out of existence or shut down by righteous ISPs ... "

"What makes you think that?" Jess thought of Dale Spender. *Women of Ideas and What Men Have Done to Them.* She thought about Sieghart and the rape and death threats women receive merely for ... speaking.

"Because on many social media sites, images of pornified women are permitted, but not of breast-feeding women. Posts about erectile dysfunction remedies are permitted, but not about contraception or abortion."

"Hm. That definitely indicates a bias."

Shane made a list of her favourite blogs and started saving what she could. Often by painstakingly copying page by page onto a flash drive. Many of the blogs had been regularly visited by brilliant women and the comments were as insightful and as illuminating as the blogs themselves.

"Give me half your list," Jess said.

So when Jess saw a notice about a new feminist club, she told Shane and they both went to one of the meetings.

As soon as they walked into the room— All of the women present looked like pop stars or cheerleaders or models … And the men present were grinning like idiots. Curious, they stayed and listened. Feminism was all about empowerment, they heard. And apparently one's sexuality was the best route to empowerment. Women could do anything if they had a man's attention. They could get anything. Jess snuck a glance at the men. Still grinning like idiots.

Jess had to admit that male attention was prerequisite. Given. She also had to admit that the only way to get male attention was to be sexually attractive. Still. But— feminism?

Shane left within minutes of arriving, but Jess stayed, listening while the women discussed with no small excitement what they'd be wearing for the upcoming SlutWalk, several nodding with approval to the occasional suggestion given by the supportive men. It was an annual event intended to make the point that women could wear whatever they want; attire did not indicate consent to sexual activity. In principle, Jess agreed. But we *do* send signals with our clothing, he thought. There were both official and unofficial uniforms: doctors, nurses, police officers, judges ... those associated with various subcultures ... So *didn't* so-called slutty clothing signify an openness to sexual interaction? The short skirts, the sheath skirts, the skirts with slits up the side or one up the back, the high heels, the push-up bras, the falling-off-the-shoulder tops, the blazing red lips, the come-hither eye make-up ... It all screamed 'Fuck me!' That's certainly what he'd thought.

And what did these women think would happen when they screamed 'Fuck me!' all day? To their treatment, their opportunities ...

And there was something else— Ah. It was being a tease. Men were so affected by the visual—didn't the women know that? It was cruel to walk around with your tits and ass hanging out and *not* be sexually available. And yet the men seemed to support it. It was ... titillating. Yes, he remembered the background thrill of being constantly aroused ... It made you feel good, it made you feel strong— Which meant it wasn't about *female* empowerment at all. She too left.

He ducked into the washroom on his way out, and saw, as always, several women leaning in to the mirrors— All the primping, the fussing with one's hair, with one's face, with one's clothes ... Hair's bad except on your head. Fat's bad except in your boobs and your ass. Wrinkles are bad all over. It's an impossible standard to meet without a lot of artificiality, and procedures that were time-consuming, painful, expensive, and downright dangerous. Why didn't women see this? Were they so desperate to get and keep the attention of men? Did they not know that most men would fuck anything that moves? And even if not, what have they done for us lately?

"You know," Jess said when she got home, "most men are psychopathic dicks, partly because that's the way they're socialized and they haven't thought much about it. But most women haven't thought much about the way they've been socialized either."

"True," Shane had no trouble agreeing. Even though Jess was the one taking gender studies, Shane seemed to be the one with the analyses. Jess assumed it was because of her lesbian friends, and she was right. Theory was one thing; application, another. Reading was one thing; recognition, another. But she'd assumed that lesbians in general were more politically astute, at least in terms of sexism, and in that, she was wrong. As Shane had once pointed out, sexual orientation was no indication of ... awareness.

"But," Shane continued, "men are socialized to hurt each other and women are socialized to hurt themselves."

Ah. Once again, she'd nailed it. Women are socialized to hurt themselves, psychologically, physically— In so many ways, women are socialized to sacrifice themselves, for others.

"And that's why," Shane concluded, "men are more ... problematic."

One weekend, while both Jess and Shane were working, there was some construction noise from the apartment building next to them. It was horrendously loud. Beyond table saw and nail gun loud. Compressor? Portable saw mill? They tried to shut it out, but after a couple hours, they were both frazzled to the bone. Suddenly the noise increased in intensity. When they looked out, they saw that the windows facing them had been opened.

So they went over together to ask how long the noise would last and could they at least close the windows for the duration. They'd decided that they would just give up and go biking or something, depending on the answers to their questions.

When they walked into the open apartment in which the work was being done, one of the men—they were all men, Jess noticed—and wouldn't've noticed before—stopped and turned to them. Shane nodded to the nearby machine, and he switched it off. The quiet was … The way their bodies immediately relaxed was palpable.

"Hi," she said, amiably, "we're in the apartment just next door, trying to work, and the noise is—well, loud. Is it going to be all day or all weekend or what?"

"And whichever," Jess added, "could you at least close the windows facing us?"

The guy just grinned at them. As if, what? They were kidding?

Annoyed, Jess said, "We asked you two questions. Could you answer them? Instead of just standing there grinning at us?"

Oh, that pissed him off. He turned his back, switched the machine back on, and resumed his work.

Defeated, they returned to their apartment, but as they were getting their stuff together, to leave, the noise suddenly diminished. They looked out, saw that the windows had been closed, and saw Brad, one of the other tenants in their building, coming back from where they had just been.

"What the fuck!" Jess fumed.

"Yeah. But hey, at least they listened to him. Do you want to still leave or—"

"I want to go over and throttle the guy! I mean, what are we, just—nothing?" he sputtered.

Shane went to the door.

"Where are going?"

"Maybe Brad found out how long it's going to last."

"Yeah," Jess said. And deflated. Because this was the way it was. Now.

Toward the end of her third year, the City of Vancouver established women-only buses. Both Jess and Shane mostly rode their bikes, but on rainy days, they took the bus. Now they took the women's bus. On the one hand, they were glad. To be free of the leers and jeers, not to mention the groping hands, but really, was it necessary to *segregate* them?

"It's like making the blacks sit at the back of the bus," a young woman said. A young white woman.

"No, it's for our own good!" someone objected.

"Yeah, heard that before."

"Don't think of it as *us* being segregated," another woman spoke up. "It's the *men* who are being segregated. Because they don't know how to be civil. Pity the few mature men who have to ride in the company of Neanderthals, ready to insult and take a swing at them if they're not man enough."

Or, Jess thought, Jess knew, if they're not strong enough or tall enough. Or stupid enough.

Jess was able to get the yard work job again for the summer. But nothing had changed … And he was more and more sensitive to … so many things.

She came home one day and slammed the door.

"Had a pleasant day, dear?" Shane grinned.

"The day was bad enough. Getting home was worse. My bike got a flat, so I had to walk the last bit. Not a problem. Until some asshole waiting to make a turn honked at me because I wasn't crossing the street fast enough." Jess had *never*, before, rushed while crossing the street. Now he was expected to. Apparently, women were supposed to get out of men's way. As quickly as possible.

"And *then, another* asshole called me rude. Because I didn't wave back at him." Apparently, women were also supposed to wave at strangers.

"Well, good thing you didn't. Wave back. If you had, he probably would've taken that as consent for sex."

Jess laughed. But it wasn't funny. It was true. So women were caught between a rock and a hard place. If you were nice to guys, that's what they thought. And so you were a slut. And if you weren't nice, you were a bitch.

And, sigh, she wasn't the only one to be slamming doors. So to speak. Shane exploded one evening as they were both just reading. "Listen to this. It's by Laura Bates, the woman responsible for *Everyday Sexism*. 'My boyfriend was an actor at the time as well and he would get casting breakdowns that were long and detailed and told you about the character he was going up for and how they were shy and introverted and how they had a bad childhood experience that made them this way and so on. I once got a casting breakdown that was four letters long. It said '32DD', that was it. Or I'd get these breakdowns that said 'She's sexy, but virginal' or 'She's naive, but fuckable'."

Was a time, he wouldn't think there was anything wrong with that. No. Not true. Was a time, he wouldn't be aware of that.

Shane graduated from her three-year program and started working on her art, her website, trying to get her stuff out there ... Jess was impressed. "Let Me Entertain You" presented a shocking continuum from Shirley Temple to snuff films. "I am Eve" presented the religious view of women, or at least of Eve, blamed for getting humanity kicked out of paradise because she ate the apple—from the Tree of Knowledge, of Good and Evil, no less. When she wasn't working, she was, unfortunately, watching tv. No doubt, the two were related, as her work was, essentially, cultural criticism. Still, it drew Jess away from her fourth-year courses …

"Oh look, he put his arm around her," Shane said. They were watching the Academy Awards. Two people, a man and a woman, had tied for the prize in one of the categories. They were standing beside the podium for a picture, trophies in hand. The man had put his arm around the woman. "I'll bet he doesn't even know why."

"I'll bite," Jess said. "Why?" She tried to remember doing that. Nope.

"Why does any man put his arm around a woman?"

"Well, affection, I guess."

"Yeah, but they're strangers. He has no basis for affection. Try again."

"I don't know. It's just something men do."

"Yeah, but *why?*"

"No reason." Jess knew better. He just didn't know the reason.

"Nope. Gotta be a reason. Otherwise, why doesn't he, I don't know, poke her with his elbow? A high-five would make sense if their win was a joint effort, but it's not. It would make most sense to shake her hand, to congratulate her on winning."

"So …"

"He's a man. She's a woman. He thinks he should protect her. As if putting his arm around her protects her," Shane added with scorn.

"More likely," Shane offered a second explanation, "he's a man, she's a woman, he's entitled to her. To own her. At the very least, to touch her."

Jess saw that. It increased a man's status to 'have' a woman. And to have one visibly by your side was proof of that. Certainly putting your arm around one gave the indication she was 'yours'. But what man in his right mind would just assume that any woman standing beside him was his? It had to be more of a reflex. Men touched women. End of story. But that wasn't any better.

"If it was you, you'd glare at him until he moved his arm," Jess grinned at Shane. "Or you'd just break it."

"Damn right I would," Shane grinned back. "And it would serve him right. Trying to humiliate me in public like that. How many people do you think watch the Academy Awards?"

"Wait— How would it be humiliating you?"

"It would diminish me! Make me into property!"

"I'm not seeing that." 'Having' a woman wasn't necessarily 'owning' a woman … was it?

"Okay, what if it was you standing there beside him, having also won the award. And he put his arm around you and squeezed you like he just did her. What would you make of that? How would you interpret that?"

Jess thought about it, then admitted he didn't know. "It wouldn't make any sense. I couldn't interpret it in any way." It would be such a bizarre thing to do.

"Exactly. And if he saw me, you, that woman, as a fully autonomous human being, like he'd see any other *man*, it wouldn't make any sense for him to put his arm around any one of us and give us a squeeze."

"See that?" Shane reached out and froze the picture.

"What?"

"I swear, whenever an episode, in *any* series—and there are many such episodes— Whenever an episode even *mentions* rape, someone suggests that she wanted it."

She was right. And he'd never noticed that. Before.

But there was consent and there was *consent*. One could consent out of fear or insecurity or just plain old surrender— But men were oblivious to such nuance. He knew that. Now. Acquiescence shouldn't be, shouldn't've been, considered consent. Consent should be considered nothing short of enthusiastic assent. Why wasn't it?

(And if men wanted to avoid 'regret rape' charges, they should make the sex wonderful. Which they should in any case.)

Another evening, they were watching the news. All of the female reporters were attractive. Most of the male reporters were not. That norm may not reduce the women to their sex, but it certainly reduced them to decoration. Almost all the women were under fifty. Many of the men were not. In fact, Jess couldn't think of one newscast in which the woman was older than the man. So, whether cause or effect, you always saw an older man paired with a younger woman. As if it should be that way. And so it is. Older men seeking younger women. *And* because age confers authority, and rightly so, women are seldom seen as, so seldom considered, authorities. Not on tv, not in the workplace, not in the world at large. And all of this was old news. And apparently chiselled in stone.

The anchor introduced a clip, in which a male politician called a female politician overweight.

"Oh look who's calling the kettle black," Shane said with disgust. "We have to look like supermodels, but they can be shit ugly. And *still* get jobs, promotions, positions of power, respect, authority."

She was right. Not only could they be overweight, men could be unkempt, their hair stringy and unwashed, their shirts rumpled, their shoes scuffed, their trousers drooping, and no one would say a thing. Worse, someone would get their coffee for them. And do much of their work for them.

Another clip came on. It seemed that the more men abused women, the more they talked about rights for women. It was like his neighbours back home: the ones who drove an RV were the ones who voted green. It wasn't a contradiction, but a compensation.

Another clip. Men talking about men, essentially.

Another clip. The same. What if, she wondered, for just one year, the media reported 90% of the time what *women* were doing instead of what men are doing? Not because what women do is better, or more newsworthy, though probably it was both, but just to see how it would change our outlook, our world view. The news might be more boring. But then, hey, what does that say? About us? It probably would have less to do with money. Again … It would likely involve a lot less death and destruction. And again.

Another clip. And it dawned on him how stupid it was that most diplomats were men. *Women* were the ones with the superior communication skills. They're the writers, the *translators*, for god's sake. And of course communication doesn't involve just words. And women were better than men at reading facial expressions, body language. And who has the most experience settling disputes? *Mom. She's* the mediator, the negotiator extraordinaire. Even historically, Jess now knew this was the case: marriage was used to form alliances between tribes, between villages; the girl who became the other chief's wife was expected to be a go-between. A lot of women's talk is social cohesion work. *Unrecognized* social cohesion work, he appended with a sigh. They go deeper; men actually *avoid* any kind of psychological understanding, not only of themselves, but also of others; women actively embrace such knowledge. And *women* were the ones with the ability to compromise. They *prefer* a win-win outcome. Men love a win-lose outcome.

Of course, maybe the goal of diplomacy *isn't* compromise, but victory; maybe those involved don't want to resolve the conflict, they want to *win*. That's why, planet-wide, we spend more on weapons than food, clothing, and entertainment put together. Unless of course you consider weapons to be entertainment. Which, he knew, men do. Turn on any tv show during prime time, and nine times out of ten a gun will be fired in the first five minutes. Food and clothing that could be used in mediation … Well, no, most conflicts weren't about food or— Actually, he thought, they were. They were about access to land, water … Even so, he thought with a grimace, when *the aliens* come, NASA's first contact team had better include a bunch of women. Because all of our weapons? Slingshots.

As for the here and now, he sighed, as long as the *other* diplomat was a man, a female diplomat would fail. She'd be ignored, dismissed, challenged, resisted, with even more vehemence than if she were a man. Because heaven forbid that a man *concede* to a woman.

And what makes it impossible to change is that any man who *does* concede to a woman, any man who *accepts* female authority is emasculated, or worse, infantilized. Because the only female authority figure he's ever had has been Mommy. So it becomes a vicious circle: no female authority figures, so no female authority figures.

But my god, if *all* diplomats were women …

Soon after, triggered by a cooking show they were watching— don't ask—he had another thought. He'd learned that whenever women enter an occupation, it becomes devalued: at one time, bank tellers and secretaries had a certain prestige—the time when such positions were held by men; schoolteachers used to be school*masters*—before women entered the classroom; and people who boast that many doctors in Russia are women fail to mention that doctoring in Russia, well, someone's gotta do it. Maybe that's why, he suddenly thought, men aggressively resist women's entry into professional sports ... He'd noticed, really noticed, how seldom women's sports were on tv ...

Conversely, well, consider cooking shows: they didn't really take off until *men* got involved. Women are just cooks; men are *chefs*. And the difference! Not simply a calm Julia Child or Martha Stewart, interesting and helpful with a new recipe, but men strutting about, screaming with self-righteous anger at their minions, rushing about with great urgency making sure every sprinkle of cinnamon is just right, because goddammit it's so frickin' important! And they call *women* drama queens. True, food preparation *is* important: doing it the wrong way can be fatal. Which makes it even more irritating that the recognition of importance didn't occur until *men* started doing it. But the men were ... *manufacturing* importance. With competition. Ah. Competition is a way to make what men do *seem* important.

So given that, Jess thought, given that the presence of women results in a loss of value, a loss of funding, a loss of media coverage, a loss of glory, if we were serious about ending war, we'd *fill* the military ranks with *women*. When becoming a soldier has about as much appeal as becoming a waitress ...

An added bonus, he grinned to himself, would be that if the enemy army were (still) male, they'd start killing themselves. Because better that than be killed *by a woman*.

On the other hand, if the enemy army were (also) female, more often than not, the war would probably just sort of fizzle out into some sort of stalemate. Women just aren't that interested in pissing contests.

And on the *other* other hand, she thought, women *shouldn't* enlist. Shouldn't've fought for the *right* to enlist. It's men, not women, who are the threat, so men, not women, should go fight. If not for men, we wouldn't need *anyone* to enlist.

"I wonder why men aren't insulted by the low standards we set for them," Jess said to Shane a short while later.

"What do you mean?"

"Well, they manage to cook a meal, and wow, they're a *chef!*"

Shane laughed. "If he changes a diaper, he's father of the year."

"If he continues to pay a child's ball game into adulthood, he gets paid a six-figure salary."

"If he gets a B.A., he's an expert in his field."

"If he writes a book full of incoherence and grammatical mistakes, he still gets published." Jess had heard about this from one of his female professors. Who'd been approached by the publisher to edit the manuscript and correct the mistakes.

"We don't expect men to pick up after themselves," Shane modified their litany, "to clean up their own messes, to fix the things they break."

"We don't expect them to be sensitive to other people's emotions, or even be aware of their own."

"We don't expect them to be in control of their sexual impulses or their aggressive impulses."

They sighed. Men were children. And they, men, were okay with that. Which was proof.

5

Jess graduated with a decent GPA; he could've done better, but he did well enough. He thought.

He was surprised to find himself agonizing over the job ads, trying to decide if he was qualified enough to apply. He hadn't done that before. He'd just applied for all the jobs that had appealed to him. Had he lied about his qualifications then? No, he didn't think so. But then … ? Ah. He'd just assumed he was qualified. Wow. *Really?* The arrogance.

In the end, he made so many calls. He filled in so many applications. He sent off so many resumes.

He was flabbergasted every time he didn't even get an interview. Especially when the position was well below his qualifications and experience. Often his application wasn't even acknowledged.

"The bar is so much higher," he said to Shane. "Now."

Shane nodded.

"It's like I have to have a fucking doctorate before I can even become an assistant something."

"No," Shane said, "if you had a doctorate, you still wouldn't be hired for an assistant position because then they'd say you're overqualified."

"But all the jobs I'm qualified for—"

"Are occupied. By men. Underqualified men."

Jess stared at her. She'd said it so … matter-of-factly.

And when he *did* get an interview, it felt … wrong. He was too forward, too pushy … In fact, one interviewer suggested, rather harshly, that maybe she should work at the company for a while before presenting suggestions for improvement. The man was absolutely right. But it felt … You research your potential employer, show them that you've done that, and present a few new ideas, to show your initiative, your keen interest— It was standard operating procedure. For men.

Another interviewer was indignant when he tried to negotiate the offered salary. (She remembered too late, from reading Sieghart, that women who negotiate their starting salary are twice as likely not to get hired.)

Near the end of another interview, he was asked if he wanted kids.

"What?"

"The last three women we hired—" The man stopped, seeing his colleague shake his head.

"Would you ask that question if I were a man?" Jess asked.

"Well, no, because—"

"If I were a *good* man, I'd want paternity leave."

They were silent.

"Furthermore," she knew she'd blown the interview, "for your information, men and women leave their jobs at the same rate. In fact, male managers leave *more often* than female managers." (It was another of the things she remembered from reading Sieghart.)

He refused the first two offers he received— Shane expressed surprise at his language: you don't get 'job offers'—you either get the job or you don't. But— Ah. As a man, things were offered to you. W omen took what they could get. It was horrifying, the difference he kept slamming into.

He turned down the first two ... possibilities, because the pay was so insulting. (It was one thing to read, as he had in Valian, that a B.A. contributed $28,000 to a man's salary, but only $9,000 to a woman's salary. It was another thing to be faced with that discrepancy.) Then he realized that that was as good as it was going to get.

A few months later, desperate, he accepted a part-time position. Kicking himself about saying no to the two full-time jobs he could've had. He had to ... what? He had to get used to being in a female body, and being treated accordingly. You'd think by now— Apparently not.

Of course, the income from the part-time job—less than 50% of what he had been expecting—wasn't enough for rent, let alone everything else, so he had to get a second part-time job. He ended up working full-time, but since each job was part-time, there were no sick days. No medical. No dental. No pension.

Worse, as a part-timer, he was clearly a second-class employee. His input was completely ignored. In fact, it seemed resented. He wouldn't be entitled to any sort of seniority no matter how long he'd work there. There were no steps up the ladder to positions of higher income and greater responsibility. Because for part-timers, there was no ladder.

At least, he thought it was because he was a part-timer. He was, of course, wrong. Very wrong. (And yes, she should have known. Having read Sieghart and Valian and so many others ...)

Most part-time positions were filled by women. Which begs the question: was part-time work devalued because women did it or were women shunted off into part-time positions because such positions were devalued? Probably both. Around and around …

One day he happened upon a website for a small company of composers specializing in music for dance troupes: all four composers were male. (He noticed that. Now.) And he remembered a male friend of Shane being surprised at all the pieces she was creating: he'd confessed confusion at the idea of creating something just because he was passionate about doing so; everything he'd created had been a course requirement, and now he was actively looking for indie film gigs, video game gigs, and what have you—gigs that paid. And a new answer to the question, Why aren't there any great women Xs, occurred to Jess. Until then, the answer to that age-old question seemed to go to merit and/or opportunity. He thought, now, that it went to employment.

Because how many men make important discoveries on their own time at home? (Apart from Ben Franklin with his kite.) All those great men, who we know to be great because of the prizes they win, the fame they garner—they get those prizes and that fame for just *doing their job, for doing whatever it is they do 'at work'.* That's where they have access to resources, an office, a lab, a studio, assistants … And simply put, women don't get those jobs. At least, not nearly as often as men do.

And even if a woman *were* to do something great on her own time at home, no one would recognize it as such. Not only because it was done by a woman, but because it wasn't paid for. Consider the distinction between amateur and professional: the difference isn't quality, it's money. That is to say, pay doesn't follow value; it precedes it. And men, more than women, get paid for their work. Around and around.

Show me two composers, he thought, one a man and the other a woman, and I'll bet it's only the man who thinks to get some buddies together and form a company (and then get paid for their work). And why is that? Because the woman thinks 'I don't know how to *form* a company ...' The man either thinks he does, because men know everything, or he knows someone who knows someone who does, or someone steps forward and says, 'Hey, you should form a company ... '.

So he talked to Shane, suggesting that somehow she get paid for her work. She had continued with her part-time job at the gallery, hoping it would become full-time, and she had continued creating brilliant stuff and posting it on her site and YouTube ... for free.

"How?" she asked, with some frustration. "I don't want to put ads on my site. I don't want to charge people to hit 'play' and see the work. I *am* trying to get my work into galleries that present this sort of thing, but ..."

Yeah. No one was interested. In *her* work. Around and around.

Just when Jess started to think that his degree in Psychology and Gender Studies was completely useless—something he couldn't quite get his head around, given, well, the world—he stumbled across notice of a new organization, a research and advocacy institute. He sent his resume immediately. Even though no positions had been advertised.

He received an email, almost the next day, scheduling an interview for the following week. Yes! He was scheduled to work on the afternoon in question, but he gave his shift to a co-worker. He could hardly afford to lose the money, but he couldn't afford to lose this opportunity either.

There seemed to be some hesitation when she showed up, and she realized they'd thought he was a man. Jess. Even so, they proceeded with the interview, but it was clear … She wasn't optimistic.

Surprisingly, perhaps fearing who knows what, they hired him. Her.

It was an entry-level position, but he was ecstatic. Then disgusted that landing such a position would make him so happy. Then surprised at his disgust. He had just a B.A. And no experience. Why had he thought that an entry-level position was beneath him?

The position paid only 70% of what he was used to. He'd thought, he'd supposed, that after graduation, he'd get an apartment of his own. A condo, maybe. Talk about dreaming in technicolour. Fortunately, Shane was happy to continue their current arrangement. And it wasn't a bad apartment. It was just that— He knew now why so few women lived in condos. Why so many lived in crappy apartments. Why eventually buying a house was out of the question. Had he thought it was their choice?

Again, he should have remembered his course material, but … It wasn't quite real until now. And it was crazy, the income differential. Did people think that women didn't have rent to pay? Did they think when they checked out at the grocery store, the cashier said 'Oh you're a woman, you don't have to pay for your food!' Ditto at the gas station? Did they think that women weren't billed for their electricity, their phone, their internet access …? That when they had to take their car in for repair, the garage, instead of charging more than they charged men (yeah, that was another thing …), charged less? Or nothing at all?

"When my sister got married," Jess said absently one day when she was making a smoothie, "she got a fridge. When I moved out, all I got was this hand-me-down blender."

"Yeah, but there wasn't a man attached to the blender. You got the better deal. By far."

Jess laughed. "Still."

"Yeah."

And although 'entry-level' suggested that he could, would, be moving up the various levels, he never did. She was never offered door-opening opportunities. He started asking for them, providing reasons as to why he should be granted such opportunities, but that seemed to make things worse.

He was never offered a raise. After a year of doing what he thought was an excellent job, he asked for one. She was told that she was already making the maximum for the position. Okay, how could he get into a higher-paying position? She couldn't.

One day she discovered that Jason, who'd been hired at the same time she'd been hired, had been moved up.

Another day, she was startled to see in the hall someone who'd been in one of her fourth-year classes. He was, she'd thought, a bit of a dick. But she discovered that he'd been hired as an assistant to her supervisor. What the hell? In fact, most of the young men in her class, none of whom had better grades than her, had found better jobs. Of course, 'found' wasn't quite the right word ... Women have to knock (and knock and knock) on the front door. Men are ('Psst! Over here!') let in the back door. Men give each other informal advantages all the time. Bros over hos.

When a recent hire was asked to check her work, she almost quit. The recent hire was a guy.

And then there were all the small day-to-day frustrations ... He was annoyed when he discovered not sabotage, exactly, but ... The men around her seemed to be provided with the necessary resources, including information, to do their tasks. She had to ask for what she needed. Often more than once. Because her queries, to everyone, about anything, went unanswered more often than not. So she had to ask again. And when she did finally get an answer, it was brief. As if she wasn't worth their time. He used to be offered information without even having to ask for it.

Sometimes she didn't ask for something because she didn't know it was available. How would she? (She sometimes felt they *intentionally* withheld information, resources, then laughed at her failure. But of course, she couldn't know for sure.) Once she discovered that someone else was provided with a complete email list for a certain task. She'd been painstakingly extracting the email addresses from another file. No wonder it took her longer to complete the task! No wonder she made more mistakes!

He stormed to his supervisor at that point, demanding to know why he hadn't been given the email list. The man looked at her as if he couldn't quite place her, as if she wasn't even on his radar.

"No one helps me anymore," he muttered to Shane after a particularly difficult day.

"What do you mean?"

"Before, I don't know, it just seems that ... Guys would compete with each other, but we also gave perks to each other. Advice. Tips. We were on the same team. Unless we weren't. It's hard to explain."

"No, I get it," Shane replied. "Now you're in the bleachers. And expected to stay there."

Paradoxically, he became so tired of men always offering to help him. Most of the time, he didn't need any help. So it was an insult. And they knew it. They were just saying 'I'm competent; you're not.' If they really wanted to help, they would've taken him seriously in the first place and provided the information he'd asked for, the resources he'd needed. So, actually, it wasn't really a paradox …

One evening, they watched a TED show, in which a 'transwoman' was describing what happened when she went to a bike shop. The young guy had said 'Can I help you?' She said, 'Yeah. Can the frame of an older Gary Fisher mountain bike start to flex and bend enough that it causes the rear brake to rub?' He replied, 'Well, disk brakes need regular adjustments.' She said, 'I know that, and in fact I do regular brake adjustments.' He said, 'Oh, well, then your rotor's bent.' She said, 'Yeah, my rotor is not bent. I know a bent rotor.' With condescension, he then said, 'Well, what do you want me to do?' She said, 'You could answer my question.' And then she said to the audience, 'This happens all the time now. I have to go three or four rounds with someone before I get a direct answer!'

"Tell me about it," Shane said.

Jess looked over at her, startled. Because yes. What 'Paula' had described. That was it. Exactly. His life now.

But— Jess struggled to— There was something more … Ah. "She's not angry about it." James Baldwin came to mind: 'To be a Negro in this country and to be relatively conscious is to be in a rage almost all the time.' "She's amused."

"Yeah, well, she hasn't had to deal with that shit all her life."

Again, Jess was startled. For a second, his life, his new life, his future, flashed before him. And—

'Paula' went on to describe another incident. When she boarded a plane, she found someone else's stuff on her seat. She picked it up to put her stuff down, and a guy said, 'That's my stuff.' She said, 'Okay, but it's in my seat. So, I'll just hold it for you until you find your seat, and then I'll give it to you.' He said, 'Lady, that *is* my seat!' She said, 'Actually, it's not. It's my seat. 1D.' He said, 'What do I have to tell you? That is my seat!' She said, 'Yeah, it's not.' Then the guy behind her said, 'Lady, would you take your effing argument elsewhere so I can get in the airplane?' And then she said to the audience that she had been absolutely stunned. She had never been treated like that as a male. Before, she would have said, 'I believe that's my seat,' and the guy would have looked at his boarding pass and said, 'Oh, I'm sorry.'

"She was 'stunned'," Shane said with disgust. "That's how little men know of sexism, of what it's like to be a woman in our fucking men-are-gods society."

Jess didn't say a word. Because Shane was right. Absolutely right. Men have no idea.

A week later, when he walked into the lunch room, he saw a guy just staring at the coffee maker. "Does this need a bag or something?" he asked Jess.

"Filters are in the cupboard," Jess replied. Tersely.

The guy opened the cupboard and took out the plastic sleeve of filters. "And you put coffee into one of these, right?" He looked around, helplessly. "And the coffee is …?"

"In the cupboard."

The man opened the cupboard and took out the coffee. He continued to stare at the machine. "There's a trick to opening it, right?"

"Oh for fuck's sake, what is your problem?" Jess all but shouted. "You've been drinking coffee for how many years? And you haven't yet figured out how to work a coffee maker? It's a fucking coffee maker. No more difficult to operate than a lawn mower."

The man stared at her.

"So I ask again: what is the problem?"

"What?"

"I'll tell you what the problem is," Jess sighed, angrily. "You insist on genderizing not only people, but also appliances. In your feeble little mind, coffee makers are feminine, whereas lawn mowers are masculine. Go figure. Indoor/ outdoor? Small/big? Who the fuck knows.

"And since you're a *male*," he continued, "you *must* be masculine. God forbid you demonstrate, therefore, any competence with a coffee maker. So you feign or maintain ignorance as a way to assert your masculinity." He stared at him. "Grow up."

She left the room. Without making coffee for him.

Well beyond making the coffee, he was constantly expected, or asked, to do this or that, things not in his job description. 'Do me a favour …,' someone would say. Or 'Would you help out a bit and …' Eventually, he noticed that the guys were never approached for favours and help. Just the women. When he started saying no, 'Sorry, not in my job description,' he was reprimanded for not being a team player.

He realized then that that attitude explained, in part, women getting paid less or not getting paid at all. They're expected to help, to assist, and what they do is considered a favour. No one expects to pay them, so they themselves don't expect to be paid. He remembered then some of the guys at school, once they discovered that she marked English papers, asking her to 'go over' their papers before they submitted them. Editorial service, for free.

Men, on the other hand, *expect* to be paid. And so they are. They are the ones women help; they are the ones women assist. But take away any man's help, any man's assistants, and let's see how much he achieves, how many reports he writes, how many companies he creates and runs. Of course, in some of those cases, the women *are* paid, but they don't get any credit. For the work they've done. Their names aren't on the report covers, the Board member list ....

Femonade had said something about male success not being based on the merits of their work, about how they can shuffle papers around all day, looking busy but not doing much, and somehow still managing to get paid, promoted, elected ... being put in charge of things, including monitoring and judging others' behavior. He saw that now. Up close. And it was personal. And it seemed there wasn't a damned thing she could do about it.

When he attended meetings, as in class, he was often interrupted. He couldn't even finish a sentence. Not one damned sentence. Excuse me, I was talking. But then, Bitch. Cunt.

Sometimes it wasn't even an interruption, they just talked over her like she wasn't even there. When had she stopped *objecting* to that kind of thing?

Sometimes they pretended to pay attention, but then continued as if she hadn't said anything at all.

After one such meeting, it hit him. It was the suit. It was like wearing a magic coat. A man could put on a suit and suddenly he was respectable. Respected. No matter how much of a dickhead he was.

One day during a phone conversation he hadn't wanted to have, his mother mentioned that his father had hired Kyle. To work at his company. He hung up shortly after that news. And then he couldn't believe how angry it had made him. The injustice was just too devastating.

Business is male, she thought. Make no mistake. Everything about it smacks of the male mentality. First, the obsession with competition. You have to be #1, you have to outcompete your competition. So hierarchy, rank, is everything. As is an adversarial attitude. Thing is, it doesn't have to be that way. Business could be a huge network of co-operative ventures, each seeking to better the whole. But no, men have to be better than, stronger than, faster than—

Second, the obsession with size. Mergers, acquisitions, expansion. Bigger is better. Bigger wins. They're always talking about new opportunities for growth. Unlimited growth. They never talk about cancer.

Closely related, the obsession with numbers. Business measures success in numbers, in quantifiable units. (And, of course, the numbers must be big.) Units manufactured, units sold, profits, paycheques. It measures value in numbers. It puts a price on beautiful views. And lives. Again, it doesn't have to be that way. When some people say something is priceless, they mean it.

Derivative of the obsession with competition is the obsession with power. Power over others. Responsibility is the flip side of power, but the only responsibility business talks about is the responsibility to shareholders—to be competitive, to be big, to produce high returns/numbers. All other responsibilities are swept under the carpet and called externalities.

And of course if you're going to compete, you have to take risks. Business is all about taking risks. Yet again, it doesn't have to be that way. Safe is good. The system could be set up so risk isn't required. (Actually, as it is, it isn't: gains are privatized, losses are socialized.)

And perhaps the most dangerous: women are devalued. Half the species just doesn't count, as far as business is concerned. She'd read an article titled "On Bankers and Lap Dancers" that said that 80% of male city finance workers visit strip clubs for 'corporate entertainment'.

All of this, she realized, is why men go into business: it has what they are. It's also why business is male: they are what it is.

And the problem is that business rules the world. Because, therefore, men rule the world. Around and around. That's why we're never going to change business, we're never going to stop its crippling effect—she remembered Shane's mention of 450ppm way back when—on the quality of our lives. Until we change men.

On a more personal note, she knew that Kyle would be making easily $10,000 more a year than she was. And she knew it wasn't just because Kyle was the owner's kid. It was because Kyle was the owner's *son*.

Though, she knew now, even if he hadn't been the *owner's* son … She was in for a lifetime of seeing men with less competence, with less seniority, getting raises, getting promotions …

When it was clear that his current job was a dead end—two years and not one raise, let alone any kind of promotion—he starting looking for another job. But as soon as he saw the letter of recommendation he'd requested, he regretted his decision. It was … lukewarm. Nothing awful, just … nothing exceptional. (Sieghart: 70% of men rate men more highly than women for achieving the same.) But she hadn't had a *chance* to do anything exceptional!

Everyone seemed relieved when she left. Was a time, people would be disappointed.

The next job wasn't any better. A few months in, she was able to schedule a meeting with her immediate supervisor and his supervisor to discuss a few ideas she'd had about how to decrease the systemic sexism. Simple things like implementing anonymity into the assignment and evaluation process, but also a few more complicated things … She was actually surprised they'd agreed to meet with her. Maybe this workplace was different.

"Hello Jess, come on in …"

She entered the large corner office, with a window, of course …

Her supervisor, Bob, introduced her to his boss, Mr. Arly.

"So," he nodded to the empty chair, "tell us about this idea of yours."

She sat down, then launched into her proposal: the problems it would solve, how it would solve them, the minimal expense involved in changing things, and so on. They asked a few questions, but their interest seemed lukewarm. Then rather abruptly, fifteen minutes in, Mr. Arly stood and looked at her supervisor.

"Well, Bob, we've got to go or we'll be late for the dinner."

And it suddenly hit her. They were just putting in time. They had an event to go to, and their meeting with her was just a way to fill the time. And tick the box for Being Responsive to Your Subordinates. She'd been such a fool!

He'd experienced the same sort of thing when he'd had that part-time position, but he'd thought it was because of being part-time. Now he knew that it was because of being female. Being female-bodied. She thought back to a few interactions with her professors, her classmates, her coworkers ...

We've all been such fools, she thought. Time and time again, thinking some man was taking us seriously when all along we were just nothing. A diversion. Or worse, a means to his end.

Then she had another thought. *That's* why men accuse us of being, irrationally, man-haters. But their experience of men is different from ours. The same men who are considerate and reasonable with them are dismissive and condescending with us. So we're not being irrational. At all. Simply put, men act differently with other men than they act with women. Way differently. So no wonder men develop a totally different view of what it's like to ... live.

The next job was even worse.

'Ms. Everett' this, 'Ms. Everett that ...

"'Jess' is fine," he told them. It felt like they were rubbing his nose in it. The fact that he had a female body. When he'd been called 'Mr.', it didn't feel like ... anything. It just was.

So then they switched to '*Ms.* Everett' this, '*Ms.* Everett' that ...

"Look," she said one day. "When you do that, you're emphasizing that I'm female. That I'm subordinate. To you."

"We're doing no such thing," the men laughed.

"You *are*. And you know it," he insisted.

Whenever she approached a bunch of them, at the vending machine or the water cooler or the elevator, they stopped talking.

Silence. And he knew, he just *knew*, they'd been talking about how fuckable the women in the office were.

How did they, the women, manage to hold their heads up? Knowing that. Knowing how little men thought of them, how irrelevant their degrees, their knowledge, their competence— how utterly irrelevant it all was?

Maybe it was just as well they didn't know. And he thought, then, surely they didn't. Know how little men thought of them.

Because if they did, they'd march into the office, every one of them, with semi-automatics and just blow them all away.

Because what else could they do? Complain to HR about a hostile working environment? It was a hostile planet.

He felt like he had to prove himself over and over and over and over. Even within the same company. Reputation doesn't exist for women except as a bitch or a slut. So she could never let her reputation for good work precede her; she could never rest on her record: in every situation, she had to start over, proving her competence. It used to be ... assumed. That he was competent.

She started to think that maybe she wasn't as good as she'd thought. But he swore he was doing the same quality of work as he'd done ... before.

She complained to Shane one day about having to prove herself—

"Well, yeah."

Jess looked at her. She didn't know.

"I didn't used to."

Shane looked at her. She hadn't known.

"Oh."

Even when he *did* manage to do something noteworthy, something that would establish competence, reputation, the success didn't snowball. It was as if it was regarded as an anomaly, not a predictor of things to come. So she wasn't building a *career*. She just kept getting *jobs*.

And the next one—

He was a customer service rep, answering phones all day long. His first day on the job—his very first day—his supervisor stood behind him and put his hands on his shoulders.

"How're you settling in, Jessie?" the man asked, all friendly-like.

Jess shrugged his shoulders, hoping the asshole would take the hint.

Instead he started massaging his shoulders. Unbelievable.

Jess sat very still, then said, tightly, "Get your hands off me."

Unbelievably—or not, given everything Jess knew about men's feelings of entitlement—the guy did the same thing the next day.

So Jess turned and belted him one.

She was fired of course.

"You're a very lucky young woman," the Security guy said as he escorted her out. "Mr. Smith has agreed not to charge you with assault."

"You should charge *him* with assault," Shane said when Jess told her what had happened.

"No one will step forward as a witness. They'd lose their jobs. And pathetic as they are—the jobs, I mean—"

"Yeah."

At the next job, he did was as little as possible. His evaluations were poor. He was told to try harder. Become better. But what

110

would be the point? He would never be good enough, because he would never be judged on his competence. Better to realize this at 25, he thought, than at 40. When you're exhausted and frustrated and angry, having spent fifteen fucking years trying, and trying harder …

He was already tired of defending every little thing he said or did. He was already tired of proving himself over and over, more and more. He was already tired of fighting for every little thing he wanted. Air time. Software upgrades. Even a fucking stapler that could handle more than five sheets of paper.

She started trying to build a life outside work. She joined the Green Party, but at the very first meeting, she noticed that the men took up more physical space than necessary, sprawling over the confines of their chairs, sometimes even elbowing the people beside them.

And not only did they take up more conversational space by interrupting the few women present, they spoke slowly, they repeated themselves, they made irrelevant comments that derailed the conversation—just to hear themselves speak, she was sure.

At one point, Jess objected to something the leader said—and she was quick about it because— It suddenly— He used to take his time. He used to talk in whole paragraphs. No one would interrupt. No one would stop paying attention if he took too long.

Even so—even though she was quick about it, and almost apologetic, the man practically had a heart attack: he started shouting at her, all blustery and red-faced, aggressively jabbing his finger in the air at her … So much for that.

He joined an all-comers basketball league, but he was put off by the divisions into teams: they'd divide the star players between the two teams, then the tall guys, then the older players, and then the women. As if women couldn't be star players. Or taller than some of the men. Or older.

Worse, they typically played one-on-one, and it seemed a foregone conclusion that he'd always pair with the woman on the other team. Failing that, with the worst of the men. One night, with a thirteen-year-old.

"I'm pretty fast on my feet," he said one night, "I'll take that guy," he pointed to one of the hotshots. They laughed at her. But what he'd said made perfect sense. Women tended to have better coordination—they could even run backwards—and better endurance, so she could always be in the hotshot's face, preventing him from scoring. When the hotshots paired off with each other, they were each so intent on being hotshots, they were each left unguarded. To shoot and score all night long. He explained that. No one heard her.

So he didn't bother to explain the converse: the women, having nothing else to do, because no one ever passed them the ball, guarded each other so closely no one *could* ever pass the ball to them, so they could never shoot, never score. The few times they *did* get the ball, they took the shot, no matter how difficult. It could be the only chance they got all night. But of course the understandable misses that made them appear as incompetent as the men had assumed them to be. Around and around.

Though ... he fumbled the ball more often than he remembered doing. Ah. His hands were smaller. No fair. And of course, being a good six inches shorter, the basket was higher. Also no fair.

None of that mattered, however, because as a woman, no one ever passed to him. No matter how often he was in the clear.

"What am I, invisible?" he'd fumed one time. Yes. That's exactly what you are, she realized.

When he managed to score, once, no one high-fived him.

Another time, when Jess set a solid, and perfectly legal, pick, the other guy ran right into him and then was so enraged, he shouted "FOUL!" and actually shoved her off the court.

All in all, it was a good work-out, running up and down the court, but that was all he did. Run up and down the court. So, so much for that.

He went back to solo activities. Running. Reading. Writing letters to the editor. And he realized that that was how women become marginalized. They keep leaving voluntarily, because they're ignored and insulted. Or they get pushed out, because they're good.

He started watching more tv. One evening, watching *The Piano*, Jess was … shocked, appalled, horrified— The scene in which a man, in a fit of rage, a tantrum, cuts off the mute pianist's finger— He has *no idea* of the damage he's done, no understanding of the irrevocable loss he has caused. It *wasn't* just a finger. It was her voice, her escape, her joy— He wondered if he would've had the same reaction before. He was afraid not.

There was something very frightening about that kind of capacity to injure: to hurt with intent is at least to act with responsibility, and it shows a sort of respect for the other, an appreciation of the harm caused; but to hurt spontaneously, recklessly, casually, without even being aware of the harm—it adds deep insult to the injury. (No doubt that was why victim impact statements were so important: the victim wants the person to *know* just what he's done, to take on that burden of responsibility.) To hurt in that off-hand cool sort of way— It was psychopathic.

And most men *are* psychopathic, he suddenly realized. So many of us throw tantrums. While in an adult male body. With a gun or knife in our hands. We're immune to the influence of ethics. To a consideration of other people's rights and freedoms. Their right to be free of fear and pain. Their right to go where they want when they want. Without the risk of assault. And we're apparently too unimaginative to empathize. Or even foresee the pain we cause. It would get in the way of competing. We say 'Of course, I care,' but we don't really. We don't care very much about anything. Except our own status. So we can't possibly understand that others do. Care. Very much. About so many things. And so we have no idea about how much pain we cause when we destroy ... the world.

So, he thought back to that incident in the bus shelter, women *should* be afraid of men. Very afraid. Because most of the time we have no idea. We're that casual about destroying things.

Though, of course, often we have a very clear idea. He'd realized sadly, that men were the reason children were taught to be wary of strangers. Even when, especially when, said strangers offered help.

Jess thought again about going to grad school. Thesis: "The presence of a Y chromosome indicates psychological impairment."

One weekend Jess decided it was time to get away, go for another hike. They'd bought a used car a few months prior, intending to use it for their adventures, but they had yet to do so. Unfortunately, Shane opted not to go with her, choosing to be with her new girlfriend; Jess was happy for her, but saddened by the prospect of losing her best friend.

He considered Watersprite Lake and Elfin Lakes, simply because the names were so delightful—something, he realized, he couldn't've done before—because real men just didn't—what? But when she looked at a few videos posted online, she didn't find the actual trails quite as delightful as their names and opted for Joffre Lakes instead. A nice long drive to Pemberton, then short 10k hike with three turquoise lakes—again, something—was it that men weren't as sensitive to color or weren't *allowed* to be sensitive to colour?

At the third lake, she met Ethan. They sat for a bit and chatted, then ended up walking the whole way back together, easy in each other's company. He was trying too hard to be impressive—she just wanted to be intrigued—but he understood the impulse. The habit. They decided to get together again the following weekend for another hike. And then another. Three months later, Jess had a boyfriend.

But as soon as they'd sort of declared themselves a couple, things changed. Expectations shoved their way into their relationship. The first time they had dinner out, Ethan expressed surprise, no, disapproval, really, at her attire.

"But I always wear casual."

"Yeah, but I thought that was just because you know, you were hiking. This is different."

"And so what would you like me to wear?" He couldn't believe he even asked that question.

"I don't know, something more ... I don't want to feel like I'm with a guy."

That was interesting. Gender is rooted in men's homophobia?

Also, whenever they were out, Jess noticed that people always addressed Ethan first, often ignoring her altogether. That shouldn't've been a surprise, but— It was. It felt like a sucker punch.

He found that she had to be ever attuned to Ethan's wants and needs. This was new. And actually, now that he thought about it, it wasn't just with Ethan. He was paying more attention to men in general. And not in the way he used to pay attention to women. Nor even in the way he used to pay attention to men in general. No, this was different. Very different. It wasn't just that he had to be more vigilant, physically. About where to go and when to go there. It was that once he was there, he had to be ever watchful about the proximity of men, and the way they were acting, alert to potential problems. It was as if he was living in an occupied country and had to keep making sure he didn't inadvertently piss off one of the soldiers. He had to make sure he didn't even come to the soldier's attention.

A few months into the relationship, Ethan told Jess that she was his moral compass.

"What are you, six? Be your own moral compass." The words were out before she knew it. But she was aware of the tendency of men to force women into the role of gatekeeper, moral arbiter. At the same time, they looked down on ethics; concern for the other, caring about the other, that was for wusses.

And Ethan was constantly asking her where his keys were, where his socks were … "I'm not your mother!" Jess had shouted at him. Though even his mother should not have to keep track of his keys and his damn socks.

But when she didn't keep track of such stuff, Ethan acted like she was ignoring him. And said so. Making it sound like a reprimand. It took Jess a couple days to realize that Ethan had expected, had felt entitled to, her attention. And she'd transgressed. Hence the reprimand.

"It's not my job to look after you," he said. "You are not *entitled* to my time and attention."

He stared at her. With incomprehension on his face.

116

Another thing was the mansplaining. He would tell her stuff. Stuff she already knew. Once, they took a moonlight walk on the beach, and he started pointing out all the constellations to her, naming them. As if she were a child. As if she knew *nothing*. About *anything*. It was *so* insulting. And since so many men told her so many things, it was also so very tiresome.

"You do remember that I have a degree, yeah? And that I'm the same age as you?"

Again, that stare of incomprehension.

He reacted the same way when she asked him, point blank, "What do you want?" They had been discussing the way things were between them. Jess wasn't happy. With the way things were. She was trying to figure out whether to stay and work on the relationship—that's what you were supposed to do, right? But why? If you had to work at it, didn't that indicate that something was wrong? So why stay? Why not just move on? And why weren't *men* supposed to work on the relationship too?

Ethan's answer had been just a litany of possibilities, and she realized it was a purely intellectual response. He didn't *know* what he wanted. He wasn't that introspective.

She'd asked again. "What do you *want?*"

"I don't know," he shrugged irritably.

"Why does the question make you angry?"

"It doesn't make me angry!" he said. Angrily.

It dawned on her a bit later that the issue wasn't that he didn't know what he *wanted,* nor even that he didn't *know* what he wanted, but that *he* didn't know what *he* wanted. Men didn't have as strong a sense of self as women did. *Because* they weren't as introspective. Or maybe it was the other way around. They weren't as introspective because they didn't have a strong sense of self. Or maybe they weren't as introspective because they didn't have to constantly self-censor themselves. "Don't walk like that, don't talk like that, don't sit like that ..." as one FtM had put it in Schilt's book.

It also occurred to her why, when men said things like 'Don't make this personal', it sounded like an accusation. Like making something personal was a bad thing. It *was*. For *men*. Who want to be allowed to injure individual people with impunity. With immunity.

So if they don't have a strong sense of self, how can they have such power?

Ah. *Because* they *don't* have a strong sense of self. They're hollow. There's nothing there but the drive for sex and the drive to win. They have no feeling. And, so, no empathy. And, so, a great capacity to hurt. Others. Other selves. Because how can they assume in the other what doesn't exist in them?

"What do *you* want?" he'd asked her in frustration. "What do women want?" That he thought the two questions were equivalent stunned her. It shouldn't've.

And then something else, another conversation, made sense.

"What do you want me to say?" he had said helplessly, having obviously said the wrong thing, again. "Just tell me what to say and I'll say it!"

"I want you to say what you think!" Jess had replied. Appalled. Did Ethan not think? No. Not for himself. Not really. And like introspection, truth, honesty, was so far from the norm. For men. You say, you do, whatever it takes. To get sex. To win.

That's why men like, nay, *need*, hierarchy. They act according to obedience, not independent thought. So they need to know who to obey. Who's above them.

"And if I don't agree with it," Jess had carried on, "then I'm outta here."

"It's that simple for you?"

"Yes! Why would I want a relationship, a friendship, with someone with whom I'm not in agreement? On the important things. Maybe even on the unimportant things."

And then, talk about important things, Ethan had defended one of his buddies who'd forced himself on—raped—a woman. "Oh come on, he didn't mean to hurt her," he'd said. As if having good intentions, or at least not having bad intentions, was enough.

While Ethan had never forced himself on her, it did seem that the more—the more she stood up to him? No, that can't be right. But it was. Ethan seemed unable to experience pleasure without conquest. So the more she stood up to him, the greater the conquest. That is to say, the more aggressive the sex became.

Of course, she decided to break up with him. He hadn't wanted *her* per se. He'd just wanted a *girlfriend*. Women are used by men only as pawns in their competition for status. That explains their rage when a woman says no, or worse, says yes, then no, choosing to leave them: in both cases, the rejection causes them to lose status. Our mistake, always, is thinking it's about us. It's never about us. It's always about them.

She tried to figure out a way for *him* to break up with *her*. Otherwise, posting revenge porn would be the least of it. But she couldn't. So she just left and hoped for the best.

"I suppose you want to still be friends," he said sarcastically, leaning against the doorway as she packed the few things she'd brought to his apartment.

"No," Jess stood up. "I don't think so."

"What, I'm not even good enough for that?" He was angry. She was leaving him. It was a judgment. Of him. Of course it was.

"Do *you* want to still be friends?" she asked him.

He snorted. She wasn't surprised. Shane had said once, "Take sex off the table and see how many men will be friends with you. The answer? Zero." She'd been providing evidence for her claim that straight men saw straight women only as sexual. Sexual beings, sexual possibilities … "That's why men can't be friends with you after you break up," she'd explained. "It's not the I-love-you-too-much-to-ever-start-liking-you shit," she quoted an old 70s song. "It's because as far as they're concerned, without sex, there's no point."

As soon as Jess closed the door behind her, she heard him yell "Bitch!" Funny how men can go from 'I love you!' to 'Bitch!' at the speed of light, she thought with a grimace, and remembered one of her classmates saying 'They're either coming on to you or insulting you, there's no in-between'.

Halfway down the stairs, she heard something smash. He must have whipped something against the wall. She was surprised. She never would have figured Ethan to be the kind of guy who had tantrums. 'Course, before, she, he, never would have called that response a tantrum. She hurried down the stairs, out the door, around the corner, and out of sight.

While she was with Ethan and using condoms, she'd decided to get sterilized. The risk of leakage was not inconsequential. To say the least. She had no desire whatsoever to spend so much of her life looking after kids. (And yet, he hadn't considered getting a vasectomy …)

He'd been surprised to find resistance. She shouldn't've been. In some places, it was actually illegal, especially if you were under a certain age, unmarried, and/or did not have your husband's consent.

One doctor she'd gone to had actually snickered and then said, "So you want the advantages of sex without the responsibilities?"

Jess didn't respond, realizing only later that it was because she'd been confused, because he had asked the question incorrectly: yes, she wanted sex, and no, she didn't want the responsibility—of *children*, not of *sex*; she *did* accept the responsibility of sex—that's *why* she was sitting in his office asking to be sterilized.

The same doctor asked why she didn't want children.

"When a woman comes to you pregnant," Jess had replied, "do you ask her, before agreeing to deliver, why she wants the child?"

He didn't reply.

"And would you be asking these questions if I were a man seeking a vasectomy?"

The man got up and opened the door, nodding at her to … get the fuck out of his office.

Another doctor asked whether her parents wouldn't be upset, that she wasn't going to give them grandchildren. He implied that she had a duty; he implied that she should be ashamed.

What? She was supposed to ruin her entire life—for her parents? She was supposed to commit to a twenty-year responsibility—for them? So they could have a genetically related playmate on Sundays for a couple hours? And bragging rights? Of what? That your daughter got laid? Got knocked up?

Eventually Jess found a doctor whose only question was whether she wanted ligation or cauterization. It was a quick surgery, a quick recovery. And she felt wonderful about it. It gave her control over her life, her destiny. She loved being neutered. It was a bit of freedom from being sexed. And it was complete freedom from being reproductive. The female body, its reproductive aspect, held you hostage.

Over the next couple years, Jess met a few more men she liked, but every time the relationship solidified, the sexist dynamic interfered and ruined everything. Who does what. Who gives and who takes. He couldn't imagine getting married, being married, being some man's wife. It would mean he'd lost himself. To the expectations. To the roles assigned on the basis of sex.

Thinking ahead, he decided to try again for a summer job. Something that might turn into a year-round job. There were lots of ads for camp counsellors and youth center workers and even though they wouldn't pay very much, she applied for a few. Some of the youth centers had year-round programs as well, perhaps she could … She received a couple interviews, which went well, she thought. They were impressed with her degree in Psychology and Gender Studies, but a little dismayed that she'd had no experience working with children or youth. Fair enough. No wait, he'd gotten positions before with no experience …

One of the youth centers hired her. She was glad to finally have a job with some real responsibility, but, sigh, that fact wasn't recognized. She'd been made to feel more important when she was doing the lawn work.

Many of the youths who showed up at the center were fans of the tv show *13 Reasons Why*, so Jess started watching it, then tried to get some good discussion going. It was her opinion that the writers had missed the elephant in the room: the problem wasn't thirteen kids who'd been mean to Hannah; the problem was sexism and its many tumours—misogyny, male entitlement, male privilege, hypersexualization, objectification, the rape culture, etc., etc., etc., still rampant in our society. Feminists have for decades exposed and fought against all that—hell, they *named* most of it—but none of that was not acknowledged. Not once. Not even a little bit. It was like Jay Asher had been born yesterday and was completely oblivious to such women's voices.

It was ironic. To say the least. (Quite apart from there are no doubt hundreds of *13 Reasons Why* novels written by women. Have any of *them* been published? Made into a movie? Received great critical claim? No. But a *man* writes about what it's like to be raped, what it's like to be subjected to misogynistic shit every fucking day, well, world, PAY ATTENTION! Asher is himself a shining example of the male privilege his novel criticizes so unwittingly. Again, the irony.)

"Consider Justin," Jess said one afternoon, having suggested her thesis to a few of the girls who'd clustered around her—the boys avoided her—and that could be her next topic ... "He thinks being a man is all about getting sex, using women for sex, and bragging about it afterwards to get points, to improve his status. 'Bros before hos'—even if it means letting your girlfriend be raped because hey, what's mine is yours, and women are just property, after all. Otherwise, it wouldn't even have occurred to him that what he 'owed' Bryce could include Jessica."

The girls glanced at each other. They hadn't seen it that way.

"Bryce is the same," Beth offered.

"Worse," Kaley spoke up. "He thinks he's so cool. He thinks he knows what girls want. He doesn't know shit!"

Jess nodded. "Thanks to all the cultural messages, men can be appallingly deluded about their knowledge and their appeal. They can lie to themselves about it. Again and again."

"We gotta get some of the guys over here," Cheryl said. "Hey, Shaun, come over here! Bring your bros!" She laughed.

The boy shuffled over, his friends in tow.

"We're talking about *13 Reasons*."

"Chick flick," he scoffed.

"Really?" Jess asked. "How do you figure that?"

He shrugged his shoulders.

"Tyler's the one that creeps me out," Mia spoke up. "I mean, he doesn't do anything but take photographs, but—"

"That's doing something," Beth said. "Definitely something."

Jess agreed. "He seems to think, like so many of the other guys, that women's bodies are public domain. Therefore, photographs of women's bodies are public domain. It's not like there's a person inside or anything."

"Which is so wrong. Guys post snaps of us all the time online. It's not right. They should ask our permission. It's our bodies!"

Shaun and his buddies laughed.

"You think it's funny?" Jess looked at him. "Why?"

He shrugged.

"You should criticize the girls too!" Jason said. "Jessica turns her back on Hannah as soon as she gets Alex. That's not right either."

"Agreed." Jess nodded. "Girls are taught that getting a boyfriend, a husband, being someone's girlfriend, someone's wife, is the most important thing they can do in their lives. With their lives. Given the way things are set up, they're not wrong. Women's status depends on their relation to a male."

"It shouldn't," Kaley said.

"No, it shouldn't," Jess agreed.

"Yeah, well, what do you expect? She's a *cheerleader*," Beth said with disdain. "Her actual *job* is to cheer and applaud when men do stuff."

"What about Marcus?" one of the other girls asked. "I mean, at first I liked him, but then when he and Hannah get together for a milkshake …"

Kaley nodded. "It's like he thinks agreeing to go for a milkshake means agreeing to have sex. At the very least, to have your hoo-hoo fondled in public. In broad daylight."

"And in the presence of the bros you brought along to witness your conquest," Jess added.

"And then when she objects, he's so … "

"Outraged," Jess supplied the word she was looking for.

Kaley nodded.

"And why? Because he feels *entitled* to touch her. As a man, he feels entitled to touch any woman. Any time, any place."

"Not all guys are dick-jocks."

Jess grinned at the red-haired boy. Terence? She hadn't heard that word before.

"So … Clay?" Jess prompted.

"He thinks he's a frickin' knight in shining armour."

"But at least he's trying to … fix things."

"But he's doesn't understand— What you said. The elephant in the room. Jessica does a much better job, addressing that. Eventually."

"But why should *she* address that. If it's the guys who are doing wrong, *they* should address that!"

"But— Something I don't get— Why didn't Hannah just get out of the hot tub? At Bryce's party? I mean how passive *is* she? She needs to take some responsibility for her actions too."

"She didn't want to be rude. She didn't want to hurt his feelings."

Beth turned to Cheryl, her eyebrows raised so high they were about to fly off her forehead.

And before Jess could quote Kate Manne—"Why, and how, do we regard many men's potentially hurt feelings as so important, so sacrosanct?"—

"Maybe she thought— I don't know," another girl spoke, "maybe she thought it would be worse if she tried to leave."

"Maybe, but— She wants Clay to kiss her. Why doesn't she just kiss him?" Jason was genuinely confused. "She wants him to ask her to dance. Why doesn't she just ask him? She tells Clay to go away, but then expects him to stay."

"Yeah, I really hated that scene," Jess said. "Remember what Tony said about it later? 'She asked him to go, he should go, end of story.' Or something like that."

"What I want to know is why did she even get into the tub in the first place? With just her bra and panties on?" Shaun glared at the girls.

"You're blaming *her?*" Beth stared at him.

"Yeah. Kinda—"

"He should've asked! You know. 'Use your words'!"

"Woulda ruined the moment," Shaun grinned.

"*What* moment?" Beth exploded. "There was nothing remotely romantic or exciting going on. If you have to tell a girl to relax, she's really not into it."

"Wasn't she wearing a bathing suit?" one of the other guys asked, puzzlement on his face. "A bikini?"

"Was she?" Shaun looked at him. He too looked puzzled. "How do you tell the difference?"

"What *I* don't get is," Alyssa spoke up, "okay, Jessica was drunk, and Hannah isn't a cheerleader, but if someone can do four back handsprings, surely she has the strength and the courage to fight back at least *a little*. Why didn't we see a sober cheerleader, or two or three, bustin' Bryce's ass whenever he tried his shit?"

Part way through the summer, Jess prepared a proposal for the year-round program, hoping to be considered for the position of Assistant Program Director, should it become vacant. The Director to whom she submitted the proposal seemed angry when she handed the slim sheaf of papers to him.

Puzzled, she mentioned it to Shane that evening.

Shane was not surprised. "'Any overt display of female agency automatically calls down violence.' Sarah Henstra. *The Red Word*. You should read it."

Jess made a note.

"But why?" She tried to remember anything like that from her courses.

"The ability to control women is high currency for men," Shane replied.

"Ah. Right. That's why they go ballistic when their wives or girlfriends do stuff without them. Anything but girl stuff. Not because it hurts them, but because it humiliates them. It makes them lose face in the eyes of other men." She hadn't thought that that would apply to non-personal relationships as well. And it didn't make sense that it did. "But how would my proposal make the Director lose face?"

Shane shrugged. Men weren't rational.

Jess saw it then. "Women aren't supposed to be competent. In any way. His superiority depends on it."

The summer ended. Jess was surprised to be asked to stay on as a youth worker. Friday nights and Sunday afternoons. She accepted. Gratefully. Because at the moment, she had no other options.

She looked once again in all the papers, at all the job boards, on all the job websites ... Again, call centers. Again, waitresses. Again, fast food places. An ad for ESL teachers caught her eye—there was a steady stream of immigrants to the west coast now—but they wanted certification. Not an actual degree in Education, though surely that would help, but at least part one of the provincial ESL certification program. Maybe she could get a job coaching conversational English without it. Or tutoring

English for university— She saw several ads for ghostwriting university papers, but decided, easily, against that. It was, as far as she was concerned, cheating. She wondered if that would have stopped him before.

She considered applying for a student loan to go back to school, but getting a job with a graduate degree in Psych or Gender Studies seemed as unlikely as getting a job with her undergraduate degree.

She came back to the ESL position. She could afford the certification course, but then she wouldn't be able to afford next month's share of the rent.

"We could sell the car," Shane said that evening when they discussed things.

"You wouldn't mind?"

"I like having it, but honestly, we don't really need it. We both use our bikes to get around, and there's always public transit. We can go back to renting a car if ..."

They thought about it overnight, then wrote and posted the ad for sale the next morning. That afternoon, Jess took it for a drive one last time.

On the way up, when he rounded one of the many hairpin turns, he saw a rockfall ahead, blocking the way. He'd been driving slowly, for the amazing views, and was well able to stop in time. He pulled over, reached for his phone to called 9-1-1 to alert them to the need for barriers and road closure signs, then remembered seeing a car in the distance behind him—

He sprinted back around the corner, surely doing the hundred in record time, then stood in the middle of the road, holding up his left hand to say 'stop' and gesturing with his right for the car to pull over. The driver ignored her. Certainly didn't slow up. Possibly sped up. Swerved around her as if she simply wasn't there.

Even as she ran back, she knew it was pointless. The explosion had been … conclusive. She called 9-1-1 again.

As she sat on the side of the road, stunned, she tried to make sense of it. But couldn't. What if there had been not a rockfall but a stalled car around the corner? She couldn't— Ah. She'd been wearing her fuchsia faux fur vest. (She *loved* that vest. The colour was so … *vibrant!*) Because it could get chilly as you got higher up. So the man—her quick glimpse had confirmed that—had assumed she was female. And if she'd been waving her arms hysterically, he might have stopped. Damsel in distress and all that. (Or might not have. No time today for some crazy lady going on about something or other.) But she'd been calm. And authoritative. Stop. Pull over.

It was one of those moments that changes everything. Only it didn't so much as change everything as confirm it beyond all reasonable doubt.

"What happened?" Shane saw immediately that something *had* happened.

Jess looked at her. Then said just one thing. The one thing— Of course because of Sieghart, Perez, Manne, Bray, and so many others, he'd suspected as much, but he didn't remember being this way, and it was just so … implausible.

"Men would rather die than listen to women."

About six months later, she discovered a lump in her breast. She immediately made an appointment with her personal physician, who confirmed the presence of a lump and referred her for a mammogram.

It was his first and he'd had no idea. It hurt like hell. Who came up with this idea? Surely there was a better diagnostic technique. No way men would even *consider* putting their penis in a vice ...

No way men would ever *have* to put their penis in a vice. Men are taken more seriously when they report pain. That's why they're given more pain medication than women. Which just added anger to the pain ...

Turned out it was breast cancer, stage zero. Her first visit to a surgeon did not go well. Jess wanted a bilateral mastectomy. Take no chances. Don't mess around with chemo or radiation, just get it out now before it develops into ... anything beyond stage zero.

The surgeon discouraged her.

"If I had a flesh-eating disease in my leg and it was likely to spread, would you refuse to amputate?"

"Of course not."

"Because I need my legs, the rest of my body."

He nodded.

"So what exactly do you think I need my breasts for?"

"Well, if you ever decide to have children—"

"Not gonna happen."

"You don't know that."

"Yes, I do. I had my fallopian tubes cut and cauterized, so unless someone kidnaps me and forces me to undergo surgery that would reverse that, not gonna happen."

The surgeon reconsidered.

"But surely, being a woman, you'll want—"

"You don't know fuck all about being a woman." And neither did I, he was tempted to add. "And you apparently don't know what *this* woman wants. Even though I've told you in plain English. Are you deaf?"

The second surgeon encouraged reconstructive surgery. Jess had read that the mastectomy itself was considered minor surgery. Piece of cake, really. It was the reconstructive surgery that was the problem: it increased the pain, the chance of infection, the recovery time, the outcome. Quite apart from running would become more enjoyable if she were just flat-chested.

"No thanks," she said.

"Are you sure?"

"Why do men always doubt women?"

"What?"

"You heard me."

And why, he wondered, do they always say 'What?' Because they didn't hear what had been said. Because they weren't really listening. Or because they heard it but didn't bother processing it. In one ear and out the other.

The man referred her to a psychologist. "Just to be sure you've considered all your options," he said. He wouldn't accept her decision otherwise.

What the fuck!

Why was being visibly female more important than, say, being a runner? Why was the pleasure of her own body, to herself, not the only criterion? Because sexism depended on the gender binary, on males being men and females being women.

It reminded her of the history of abortion. First, women weren't even permitted to have an abortion until the woman had had at least one child. Must fulfil the female role first! Even if it was life-threatening. And pregnancy, then birthing a child, was indeed life-threatening. Second, even when abortions were permitted, you had to go through a psychological assessment. You had to prove, to a committee, that you were incompetent, that pregnancy would cause significant emotional distress such that you might harm the child, or yourself, in order to get an abortion. It was bizarre. Wouldn't they want you to prove, instead, that you were *competent*? To make the decision? It was as if the men—for it was men who were in charge of providing the abortions—thought women were incapable of having wants (wanting *not* to be pregnant), of making reasoned choices (choosing not to be a parent), rational decisions. Or, more likely, it was as if a woman's wants and choices were irrelevant. Because if she *were* competent, then her decision should be accepted. It's as simple as that. Of course, if she were incompetent to be a good parent, her decision should be accepted as well. Which begs the question, why were there TACs, Therapeutic Abortion Committees, in the first place?

The third surgeon, a woman, supported Jess' decision. Encouraged it, in fact, as the safest course of action. A bilateral mastectomy was scheduled immediately.

That evening, Jess confessed to Shane that she was looking forward to it. To being flat-chested.

"Do you really hate being a woman that much?" Shane asked.

"No, it's not—"

"You don't like your body."

Well, that was true. He *wasn't* thrilled with the female body: the large breasts, the wide hips, the monthly menstruation, the being shorter than almost every man alive, the almost total absence of muscle definition ... But truthfully, he hadn't been thrilled with the male body either: he certainly didn't miss his stuff being on the outside, he didn't miss the surprise erections, he hated having a moustache, he hated having a beard, but he also hated having to shave every damn day ... So she didn't want to be male again. She just didn't want to be female.

"Not completely."

"Does anyone? Completely?"

"Probably not. So what's wrong with making modifications? You've gotten a tattoo. People get holes put in their ears all the time. And face lifts and tummy tucks … Isn't a mastectomy just the flip side of breast enlargement? And somewhere on the same continuum as getting sterilized? Honestly, if I could have gotten my uterus removed while I was at it— It's not so much that I hate being female. I hate being reproductive.

"I think," she continued, "that my ideal body would be a sort of neuter, androgynous, lean, muscled but flexible, body."

"Like the aliens being kept at Roswell," Shane grinned.

"Well, a bit bigger and more muscled than that. And without the huge head. That's gotta go."

What he really hated were the expectations that came with being female. Being feminine, which meant … so many things. But he didn't have to comply with those expectations. And mostly, he didn't. And he hadn't been thrilled with masculinity either, the whole macho thing … Then too, he'd simply chosen not to comply much of the time. He remembered, now, being called a sissy or worse—but something equally 'female'—just because he'd just opted out of the relentless competition.

"I actually like being female," Jess said. Realized.

"I'm more sensitive—to tastes, to scents, to colours … It's a richer life.

"I'm more introspective. So it's a richer life in that respect as well.

"It would explain a lot. Men's low sensory perception and lack of introspection. It would explain why men value things only in terms of their use. Trees. Women. They don't see any aesthetic value. They don't consider any intrinsic value, any autonomy in the other. They see only instrumental value.

"But all that might also be because of the culture. Because certain aspects were allowed, even nurtured, not discouraged with a baseball bat."

"Could be both," he agreed.

Then continued. "Tears and laughter come more easily. Anger and affront came less easily. My emotional intelligence seems higher. Maybe because my emotional range is greater. Used to be if I was disappointed, I got angry; if I was hurt, I got angry; if I was sad, I got angry."

"Wow. Really?"

Jess nodded.

"I don't know whether I actually *have* a greater emotional range now or whether it's just that I can distinguish between the various emotions now.

"Either way, and because of the introspection I mentioned, I can imagine that others have as rich a life as I do."

"That just sounds like maturity," Shane said.

"Well, honestly, I do feel more mature. As a woman."

"But that could be the result of sexism. Not biology. Or chemistry. Or whatever. At least with respect to maturity manifesting itself in responsibility. Men make women responsible for their behaviour. So— Hm. Adults are responsible for kids' behaviour. Could they be connected?" Shane grinned.

He did not dispute her implication.

"Words come more easily now," Jess continued.

"We do know," Shane conceded, "that when women who transition get testosterone, there are actual changes in their brains. The amount of grey matter in the areas responsible for language processing shrink."

"Really?" He was happy to hear there was physical evidence for his experience.

After a moment, he continued. "But it's not just the sensory differences and the introspection differences and the emotional differences and the verbal differences— There's something *else*. Or maybe it's *because* of all that. Life isn't as black and white. In general. I feel like I have access to the whole spectrum now, not just the extremes. I'm more aware of nuance, all the in-between."

Jess continued. "I remember reading an account by a woman who transitioned. Before doing so, she'd spend forty-five minutes debating which pasta sauce to buy, which vegetables were the freshest. Now she just grabs some. She says she's more decisive, but I say she's more … simple. Less complex. Less aware of … the in-between.

"You know, I've come to see, to think, that our world is crass. Superficial. Mediocre. There's no subtlety, no depth. It's two-dimensional. We've replaced making love with having sex. We've replaced friendships with social media sites. Too few seek beauty, insight. Too few aspire to intelligence, knowledge."

"Too few *value* beauty, insight," Shane added. "Too few *value* intelligence, knowledge."

Jess nodded. "We are impoverished. In every way. And now I know why."

Shane nodded. She knew what was coming.

"It's all because men dominate. Their values dominate. And driven by testosterone, they value … all the wrong things."

After another moment, Jess changed direction slightly.

"A lot of what I like about being female is the stuff I *don't* feel. I like not thinking about sex all the time. I like not feeling sexual all the time.

"I like not feeling so … driven. I like not feeling like I have to be *doing* something all the time. I can slow down. I can stop. I can sit still. I can relax. I can be quiet. I can *enjoy* sitting still, relaxing. I can *enjoy* the quiet.

"I like not having to spend so much energy trying to control myself.

"I like not having to posture all the time. I like not having to bullshit my way through life."

"And you think all that is because of being female?"

"I do. I think it's because I've got estrogen rather than testosterone coursing through my body. And I'd much rather have estrogen.

"Hm."

"Thing is," Jess continued, "I'd rather be treated like a man."

Shane groaned.

"Most of the time. I mean, being treated like a woman *by women* is better. In a lot of ways. This conversation, for example. And every conversation we've ever had. Would *never* happen between men."

Shane nodded.

"But otherwise, it's like I'm invisible. I'm here, but no one sees me. I speak, but no one seems to hear me. I used to— I didn't used to have to *try so hard*. To be seen. To be heard. It makes me feel … insignificant. I used to feel important."

Shane snorted.

"It's true! No one ever asks for my opinion now. No matter how good my arguments, no matter how much supporting evidence I present, I have no influence whatsoever. Over anything."

"I wasn't disagreeing," Shane said.

"And when I offer my opinion anyway, I'm challenged. Every frickin' time. All day. Every day. Even on my most uncontroversial utterances, I'm questioned: Are you sure? How do you know that?"

Shane nodded.

"I also didn't used to have to try so hard just to succeed," Jess said. "It's like we're all in a pool, and the men are swimming *with* the current, but the machine in the women's lane is set so we have to swim *against* the current. Hell, some of the men are just floating around and they *still* get from point A to point B—"

"At least we're allowed in the pool now."

Jess stared at her. She was right. That didn't make it better.

"And the insults. Every day, all day, we're reduced to our sex."

Again, Shane nodded.

"Not only by the interruptions, the dismissals, and the many condescensions, not only by the endless commentary about how we look and the touching, but by outright name-calling. It takes its toll. Being called a cunt or a bitch every day."

Yet again, Shane nodded.

"I have to fight for everything: acknowledgement, respect, opportunity, autonomy, dignity … Everything I used to take for granted."

Once more, Shane nodded.

Jess grinned at her. "You'd think that after twenty-some years, I wouldn't be surprised by all this. But— It's just that—I *remember*, on some level, things being different. *So different.*"

"Actually, it's good you keep being surprised. The rest of us are, well, it's like the frog in the boiling water. The … disenfranchisement has happened so gradually, from infancy, to childhood, to—a lot of us rebel big time when we hit puberty, but then … "

Yeah.

"So … ?" Shane wondered where Jess was going, would go, with all this.

"Well, I have to say, I'm not looking forward to this being the rest of my life. I mean it's not just for a week, Monday to Friday, nine to five, like that guy, Martin, had. You know? The guy who accidentally was treated like Nicole at work?"

"Yeah. The one who, after a mere week, Monday to Friday, nine to five, summarized 'Folks, it sucked.'"

"Yeah. But— It's before and after work as well. And on the weekend. And for not just for a week, but for a month. A year. Ten years. Twenty. Forty. Your whole fucking life, every minute of every damned day, from the time you get up to the time you finally fall asleep, being ignored or dismissed; being patronized, underestimated; being doubted, challenged, resisted; being demeaned and humiliated; being completely … irrelevant … to anything, everything."

"Wow. Until now, I was kinda happy with my life," Shane grinned.

"Sorry. And yet—this will make you happy," Jess continued, "as I said before, I'd rather be female than male. Personally. Not socially. Socially, how you're treated, yeah, it sucks. But personally, how it feels, it's good. Better."

Shane nodded.

"In fact, now, if I were male, I would be disgusted with myself. I'm ashamed to have been a man.

"We feel entitled. To attention. To glorification. To physical space. To other people. To, well, everything. We are, in a word, in two words, greedy and self-centered. But that's not the worst of it.

"We are entertained, sexually aroused, by other people's humiliation. Leave it to us to turn the creation of life into a degradation. Rape.

"We enjoy hurting. We tear the legs off flies, we put firecrackers into dogs' mouths, we attach electrodes to people's genitalia.

"And we have no desire to change. Any of that."

They were beyond immature. Beyond, even, sick. Men—many men—too many men—were defective.

"So, what's the solution?" Shane asked.

He'd studied women's history. He knew they'd tried everything. Polite requests; angry demands. Educational remedies; legal remedies. And the greater their attempts, the greater the backlash.

Everything, that is, except androcide. But if women started killing men, men would start killing children. To make them stop. And it would work.

They could just wait. For the Y chromosome to completely disintegrate. For sperm to become completely unviable. But they didn't have time to wait. 450ppm, 2 degrees—one or the other likely during the 2030s.

"Speaking as a woman," Jess replied, "I don't know."

"And speaking as a man?"

www.ingramcontent.com/pod-product-compliance
Lightning Source LLC
Chambersburg PA
CBHW030804190726
48285CB00003B/1015